Two Faces

Two Faces Have I

By

Nicholas Portillo

authorHOUSE®

AuthorHouse™
1663 Liberty Drive
Bloomington, IN 47403
www.authorhouse.com
Phone: 1 (800) 839-8640

© 2002 Nick L. Portillo. All rights reserved.

No part of this book may be reproduced, stored in a retrieval system, or transmitted by any means without the written permission of the author.

Published by AuthorHouse 04/06/2016

ISBN: 978-1-4033-4098-6 (sc)
ISBN: 978-1-4259-4524-4 (hc)
ISBN: 978-1-4033-4097-9 (e)

Library of Congress Control Number: 2002092406

Print information available on the last page.

Any people depicted in stock imagery provided by Thinkstock are models, and such images are being used for illustrative purposes only.
Certain stock imagery © Thinkstock.

This book is printed on acid-free paper.

Because of the dynamic nature of the Internet, any web addresses or links contained in this book may have changed since publication and may no longer be valid. The views expressed in this work are solely those of the author and do not necessarily reflect the views of the publisher, and the publisher hereby disclaims any responsibility for them.

1

1952, Albuquerque, New Mexico
Saint Anthony's Home for Boys

Sister Clara's footsteps echoed down the long empty hallway. Her crepe-soled shoes made practically no sound but the aged oak floor amplified the whispers created by her sedate pace. Her duty at this moment was to patrol the halls and classrooms, to discourage or capture any little boys intent on escaping the supervised group of children on the playground.

Most of the 200 boys in residence in Saint Anthony's Home for Boys were orphans. Sister Clara had only recently come to the orphanage. At the age of 30 she hadn't been a nun very long. While she had been in college working on her Master's degree in music, she had fallen completely and irreversibly in love. She had been devastated when the romance ended. Her grief was so severe that her parents had reluctantly accepted her decision to become a nun. They feared that she would suffer a mental breakdown if they denied her pleas.

As Sister Clara casually walked down the hallway, she suddenly came to a halt. She listened intently to hear the soft sound of music. She walked about thirty feet further down the hallway and then once more stopped to listen. There it was again, the faint sound of a piano. As she turned to decide from which direction the music was coming, the hallway again became silent. Walking a few steps further, she could hear the sound of the piano starting again. She started walking faster toward the sounds that seemed to be coming from around the corner.

The music was getting louder and she could tell that she was listening to a novice play the piano. When she rounded the corner, Sister Clara stopped to listen again. The way the piano was being played, she didn't believe she was listening to a nun practice. This could only mean that one of the boys from her group had been able to sneak into the classroom to fool around with the piano.

As Sister Clara arrived outside the door hiding the truant child she decided not to open the door just yet so she could listen without causing the music to end. Because of her own musical education, she determined that she was listening to a young child play the piano with one hand. The boys in the orphanage knew only the religious music or songs sung in the choir or taught in the classrooms. Nevertheless, this young child had both a talent for music and a talent for playing the piano, even if he was playing with only one hand. Sister Clara knew that there couldn't be any written music in this classroom so this young child was playing by ear, meaning what he was playing was music he had only heard.

Sister Clara was interested to discover who this child could be. But she also wanted a few more minutes to listen to him before he knew that he had been discovered. Sister Clara had a smile on her face as she stood leaning casually against the wall listening with amazement. She had to give credit to this child for knowing the songs well.

After 15 minutes of listening outside the classroom the sound of breaking glass distracted her. She turned her head to the right to glimpse a baseball fly in, hitting the wall, bouncing on the floor and finally rolling to a stop amid broken glass. Running over to look through the broken window, she could see that some of the boys from her group who had been playing baseball in the courtyard, were standing below and looking up toward the broken window. A nun in the courtyard below walked over to the boys to investigate the accident so Sister Clara pulled her head back inside and decided that it was time to determine the identity of this young musician.

But when she opened the door, there was no one sitting at the piano. She walked into the classroom and carefully looked around in the hope of finding the child hiding somewhere behind the chairs or desks. That was not to be. Sister Clara realized that while the broken window distracted her, the sound had also alerted the child. She concluded that he must have looked into the hallway and when he spotted her looking out the window, he escaped down the hall to avoid punishment.

Sister Clara just stood there looking at the piano, curious to learn the name of this talented child. Now she knew that one of her young boys was interested in playing the piano and she was determined to find him. Sister Clara made it a point to walk by this classroom door at least twice a day for several of the following days, hoping that she would come across this young man who had her interest. She tiptoed through the hall just so she would not give herself away. But when she got to the door, she heard nothing. She even put her ear up against the door, just to make sure she didn't miss a sound. When time permitted, she kept checking the classroom, only to find it empty. What a disappointment for her. Now she was even more determined to find this young man. She had labeled the mysterious pianist her little phantom.

The reason Sister Clara had not heard music coming from the piano was because one day, while she had her ear up against the door, her little phantom approached the scene of the crime from behind her and had spotted Sister Clara. He then quietly turned around and walked away, never to return. This young boy knew that if he were caught in the classroom without permission to play the piano, he would be severely punished.

He didn't realize that Sister Clara was not out to punish him. She was amazed that this child was playing the piano without being forced to. She had seen many parents who had insisted that their children take lessons. But because this young man had such a personal interest to play, even without lessons, she believed that with his talent, he could one day become a great pianist.

Sister Clara had a lot of experience, education and interest in music. Before Clara Angelica Fulton took her vows as a nun, she had studied piano for 8 years. She had an ear for music and what she had heard, definitely had caught her interest. As the days went on, she kept her eyes on all the boys, trying to figure out which child could be her talented little pianist. She thought about each individual child, trying to put the puzzle together. But still she could not determine his identity.

Sister Clara had finally come up with a few names of the boys who she thought could be her mysterious phantom. Now she would keep a close eye on them, watching their every move. But little did Sister Clara know how wrong she was. Her young pianist had found another piano to play in the north wing of the building on the opposite side from his former location. Weeks had passed and still Sister Clara walked by the door where she once heard the sound of music coming from the piano that now sat alone. She still put her ear against the door, but heard nothing.

As time went by, Sister Clara did her usual daily chores, watching over the boys with the help of the other nuns. The nuns always had their hands full with the boys, having to stop fights, tracking them down in places where they were not supposed to be and dealing with other mischievous things boys got into while growing up. One boy by the name of Nicholas was a particular problem. He was not truly a bad boy, even though he had his share of fights and other scrapes. His problem was that he was usually the child who was in the right place at the wrong time. He was a loner, always seen by himself with his harmonica in his hand or in his back pocket. You could only hear him play from a distance. If you tried to get close to him while he was playing, he would stop suddenly. Nicholas was very shy and didn't feel comfortable playing in front of anyone.

At least twice a day, Nicholas received punishment for getting into trouble. He was spanked with the paddle or even got a swat with a ruler on the back of his hands. One nun had taken a particular dislike to him. She was the one to use the ruler on his hands. Her reasons for this prejudice were hidden. Perhaps it was because he was always in trouble or maybe it was just an instinctive reaction on a personal level. His knuckles were already showing some signs of abuse. In 1952, punishment by paddling was acceptable and Nicholas received his share.

Sister Clara was a gentle non-violent nun. Gentle and understanding parents in an upper-class home had raised her. Punishment by paddle, ruler, or by any other means of contact to the body was out of the question for Sister Clara. She didn't understand why some nuns acted as they did. She wondered if it was just the burden of too much responsibility or if it was the way they had been raised. Being a nun did not exempt them from being human.

Taking care of 200 boys was a nerve-wracking job and a big responsibility. Some parents have a hard time taking care of one child. Sister Clara had seen Nicholas get more than his share of beatings. Any of the nuns could punish a boy from any group. They were not restricted to only the boys assigned to their own group. But because Sister Clara was one of the younger nuns, there really wasn't much she could do to change the method of punishment. Her thought was that if she could show her loathing for this type of punishment and set an example of gentle reprimands, perhaps she could influence a change in the nuns' treatment of the boys.

She glanced at Nicholas' hands and saw the signs of abuse. Sister Clara felt sorry for Nicholas. Her education on the piano had taught her the importance of hands and fingers. She cried a little inside each time one of the boys was punished. She was even more sensitive toward the punishment directed toward Nicholas because he was always getting into more trouble than the other boys were.

After months of silence from her mysterious little phantom, Sister Clara had an idea. She would gather her group of boys together in the orphanage theater on a Sunday afternoon and entertain them by playing the piano. She knew how talented her performance would be and thought that with the right music, she would get the attention of the young boy who had been eluding her. Her idea was to watch the boys' expressions as she played the piano. She knew that the young boy she was searching for had a talent to play by ear and hopefully he would watch her motions closely. She felt that she would be able to discover his identity by his interest in the music. Sister Clara already pictured in her mind this young man's reaction.

Sunday finally rolled around and Sister Clara gathered her group of boys in the theater. In the orphanage, the boys were grouped by certain ages. Sister Clara had charge of the younger boys ranging from 6 years of age to 8 years of age. She would not entertain all 200 of the boys, just those in that age group. She had two other nuns helping her with a group of 50 boys. The only time all age groups got together was for the Sunday mass or for other very special occasions.

Sister Clara had arranged for the boys she suspected to be interested in her performance to sit in front of those she had eliminated from her possible choices. In this way, she would have a closer look at them while she was trying to pick out who might be the elusive phantom. There was one problem. She had not really decided how to approach the boy when she discovered who the little musician was.

After all the boys settled in their arranged seats, Sister Clara started performing. Her eyes focused on the boys that she had selected to sit in front. She had not played the piano in the orphanage before because she was fairly new to the home and they had other nuns who had been responsible for playing the piano. This would be Sister Clara's first program. She thought that 15 minutes of playing time would give her enough time to pick the young musician out of the crowd of boys. The two nuns with her were amazed at her talent. She played several lively tunes that had the attention of all the boys.

Still, none of them had the expression she was looking for. Her last selection was a semi-classical piece. Her performance was so moving that she practically had the other nuns weeping with emotion.

Several of the boys did appear interested in her music. She thought that they were possible candidates but she recognized the desperation in her choices. Deep down, she had an instinctive feeling about this child. These boys did not have the special look she was hoping to see on the face of her phantom. She knew that the semi-classical piece of music would be too difficult for the boys to understand. But she also knew that it would have livened up the face of the young pianist she was looking for. If any of these boys had as much interest as the child she had heard playing, this semi-classical selection should do the trick.

As she looked into the faces in front of her, she had a deep feeling of disappointment. Sister Clara didn't know what had gone wrong or why she had failed to bring forth her mysterious little phantom. Her performance had ended and other groups of boys started to enter the theater.

Sister Clara decided to run down to the nuns' lounge to take a moment's break. On her way to the lounge, she had to pass by the infirmary. As she passed the open door of the infirmary, she turned her head and could see a child lying on one of the beds. Sister Clara was curious about which of the boys was sick so she entered the infirmary to see Nicholas lying there. She had been so caught up in trying to find her mysterious little phantom, that she had not even realized that Nicholas was absent from her group of boys in the theater.

She could see that Nicholas was sweating. She wondered if he had caught the flu that had been passed from boy to boy. How could such a small child look so innocent and be such a handful at the same time? He was always getting into trouble of some kind. She started to think back to one of his mischievous incidents. He had crawled through an open window into a room where potatoes and apples were stored. The home used these items to make their own potato chips and apple sauce. Nicholas was caught frying potatoes using the bottom part of an empty can as a frying pan. Sister Clara chuckled as she wondered how Nicholas could have gotten such an idea. Nicholas received his usual punishment for that little escapade.

As Sister Clara was thinking about all the mischievous things Nicholas had done, he was lying on the bed with his fingers twitching in his sleep. As she sat down on the edge of the bed and picked up the empty hand close to her, his other hand was clutched tightly around his harmonica. Staring at the hand she was holding, she admired his long fingers. Smiling to herself, she said softly, "Oh Nicholas, I wish you wouldn't bite your fingernails."

She held Nicholas' hand with both of hers and just sat with him, missing her break while she wished that there was some way she could help him stay out of trouble. She knew that curiosity always got the best of Nicholas. The nuns would try to hide the fact that they had a favorite child among the boys. Sister Clara decided at that moment that Nicholas would be one of her favorites, even if he were more mischievous than the other boys. Possibly, the reason was because Nicholas got more than his share of punishments and she felt sorry for him. Or perhaps it was that Sister Clara felt the draw of a special bond towards Nicholas. It seemed more like a mother's instinct to protect one of her children, though she had never had any experience at being a mother.

She thought of how she had heard the other nuns talk about Nicholas. One had said that she had seen Nicholas take things apart, just to see how they work. No matter what he had taken apart, he had always been smart enough to be able to put it back together. Another nun admitted that she had caught him disassembling one of the wind-up phonographs. When she asked him why he was taking it apart, he said he just wanted to see what made it turn. Sister Clara had laughed out loud when she heard that story but then realized that she was the only one laughing.

The other nun finished her story by saying that after he had put the phonograph back together she had severely punished him. At that point, all the other nuns listening to her story laughed. Sister Clara did not find the statement funny at all. Nicholas' mischievous acts were often nothing but acts of curiosity.

Sister Clara smiled when she pictured Nicholas walking around with his harmonica in his back pocket. The word among the nuns was that Nicholas could really play that harmonica well. But the only time she saw Nicholas with the harmonica in his mouth was at a distance. If you wanted to hear Nicholas play the harmonica, it was necessary to sneak up on him or catch him when he didn't know you were there. She thought it was because of his shyness. One day, Sister Clara had decided to ask him to play the harmonica for her and his face turned red from embarrassment. Nicholas just could not play in front of anyone. "What a waste, that no one can enjoy his music," she thought to herself.

More that six months had passed since Sister Clara had played the piano for her group of boys. She was doing her usual task of patrolling for wayward boys when she met Sister Jessica in the hallway. She was one of the nuns assigned to the same group of boys. Sister Clara and Sister Jessica were close in age and shared similar temperaments, consequently they had become friends.

"I heard you playing the piano this morning but I didn't have time to stop in to say hi, so I just walked on by," Sister Jessica remarked to Sister Clara. She was not as familiar with all the rooms in the orphanage as Sister Clara and did not realize that the room from where the music was coming was a vacant classroom used for storage. Sister Clara had a surprised look on her face as Sister Jessica remarked about hearing her play the piano. "What's the matter Sister Clara?" asked Sister Jessica, puzzled by her reaction.

"Oh nothing," said Sister Clara, "I just felt dizzy for a moment, but I'm OK now." Sister Clara knew that she had not been playing the piano that morning. In fact, she hadn't played for six months since that one Sunday in the orphanage theater. Then Sister Clara realized that it was possible that Sister Jessica had actually heard her mysterious little phantom. She had thought he had vanished but it seemed that the phantom was back, as he had struck again. As Sister Jessica was heading away, Sister Clara called out to her. "Which classroom was I in when you heard me? I have played in two places this morning." Sister Clara was whispering a prayer under her breath, "Please forgive me, Lord, for lying to Sister Jessica." But she didn't want Sister Jessica or anyone else to suspect anything unusual at this time.

"It is the last classroom on the right in the North wing," replied Sister Jessica.

"That classroom hasn't been used in years except for storage," muttered Sister Clara. "That explained why I haven't heard my little pianist in the South wing classroom. My clever little phantom has changed classrooms. He must have found out that I knew he was playing the piano in the other classroom. Smart child," she thought. "Now, maybe I can find out who this boy is. It seems that I have waited years to discover his identity, yet I know it has only been months. I must be very careful or I may lose my chance to discover who he is."

She planned the ultimate surprise. She was excited and overwhelmed with the prospect of ending her mystery. She made her plans so that no one was alerted, especially the little musician. For the first two days, Sister Clara did not hear a sound coming from the storage room. She was praying that the boy would not spot her, for her plans would then all be a waste of time. She believed that if she were caught waiting for him, he would find another location to practice the piano because he was determined to play, no matter what the punishment might be if he got caught.

After the third day, she decided to take a chance peek inside the room where the piano was located. Walking into the classroom used for the storage, she looked at all the desks, chairs and tables piled high, collecting dust. A beam of light shined through a cobwebbed window. Sister Clara's habit created a slight breeze that lifted the dust from the floor to swirl into the air and reflect the light. Taking more steps to move deeper into the room, the aged oak floor creaked beneath her tread.

Sister Clara wondered how a young child could enter the shadowed room without fear. She looked around to see where the piano was located. In the back of the room, barely visible above the piles of furniture, was the top of the upright piano. All of the pianos in the orphanage were of the upright type, old but in good condition. She could not see as far down as the keys. It was a marvel that this child could locate the piano behind all the stuff that was being stored there. He would have had to be part mouse to get to the piano. Sister Clara just smiled and shook her head whispering, "Now that's determination."

She was excited but she thought that if she lost him this time, she might not get another chance to catch him for a long time. Sister Clara realized that this child knew that if he were caught playing the piano, punishment would follow. He did not know that Sister Clara just wanted to help him with piano lessons.

The idea of giving piano lessons was new to Sister Clara because she had not thought that any of the boys would be interested. Now, she realized she could be wrong. She could teach this child everything she had learned and because of his young age, learning would be easy for him. She hoped he would be interested in taking lessons. Sister Clara had decided to hide in the room across the hallway. Many things raced through her head as she waited. She hoped that this was not a waste of time. She tried to assign a face to this child but could not picture who he might be.

The moments of anticipation were almost over for Sister Clara as she heard footsteps outside in the hallway. The sounds of the footsteps came closer and her heart started beating faster from the excitement. She thought that she should be ashamed of herself but decided instead that these games of hide and seek had brought out the child inside herself. She could hear the squeaky door of the classroom open, then close with caution as if an effort was made not to alert anyone who might be close by. Sister Clara listened and waited. She was so nervous she thought of Nicholas and wondered if he felt like this because at this moment, she had the urge to bite her fingernails.

It took a few minutes for the young boy to worm his way between the stacks of furniture to where the piano sat. Anticipation was eating away at Sister Clara, "Hurry, hurry," she whispered. She was afraid that she might do something stupid like fainting, creating a sound which would cause her little musician to disappear. "Now you're starting to think crazy thoughts and next you'll even be talking to yourself," Sister Clara whispered again.

She waited for the sound of the piano, planning to give the child time to get so involved with his playing that she would be able to spring her ultimate surprise on him. As this young musician played the piano, Sister Clara listened carefully to him. He had gotten a lot better in the seven months since she had last heard him play. This time, he was using both hands to play and she couldn't believe how talented he was without taking lessons. The musical selections that this young man was playing were pieces from everything that was taught in the orphanage but with a little more upbeats added and a slight change in the rhythm that sounded good.

"I never played this well when I was a beginner." Sister Clara was impressed by his progress. "I went to college to study music and this young boy, without lessons, is doing a great job of playing on an old upright piano. Not only is he playing well, but he has also learned to improvise." Her heart beat faster just listening to him. "If my heart beats any louder, he is going to hear it."

After spending about 20 minutes listening to her little phantom play, she decided it was time to surprise him. As much as she hated to spoil his concert she wanted to find out who he really was. Sister Clara was thinking, "I don't think I will ever be able to sleep again until I find out who you are." She tiptoed out from the room where she was hiding across the hall to the room where her little pianist was playing. Her hands were shaking from excitement and she couldn't quite open the door smoothly, but nevertheless, she got it opened and walked in very slowly.

Sister Clara took a deep breath and started to tiptoe slowly toward the piano, trying to get as close as possible. She knew from experience, that the wooden floor would creak if she stepped on the wrong spot. Before calling for this child to come out, she was hoping to get a glimpse of him at the piano. She wanted to see his hands and how he held his body as he played. For her own satisfaction she wanted to see the expression on his face. Unfortunately, everything was piled up too high for her to see him.

As Sister Clara worked her way closer to the piano, she picked up a ruler sitting on a desk in front of her without realizing her action. Moving still closer, she fumbled and knocked over a chair. The music stopped and silence filled the air for a brief moment. The only thing each person heard was the pounding of their own hearts. One heart was beating fast due to excitement and the other heart was beating fast due to fright. But both hearts were beating out of rhythm.

Sister Clara called out in a shaky voice, "Come out of there, young man." She still did not realize that she was holding the ruler in her hand. With her body trembling slightly, the sound of the piano bench legs scraping on the wooden floor gave sister Clara an indication that the boy was starting to make his move out of the cubby hole. The scuffle of little feet was the only thing that was heard as he worked his way toward the opening in front of Sister Clara. She was accidentally blocking his exit with her long black habit so he had no choice but to crawl out underneath her gown. This unexpected action startled her and she let out a scream and jumped to one side, getting the scare of her life. She was still unaware that she held the ruler in her hand. The young boy stood up and Sister Clara took her first heart-stopping look at the child she had been so eagerly waiting to see.

Her eyes opened wide while her jaw dropped, "Oh Lord I'm going to faint," mumbled Sister Clara and for a moment she stood frozen in a state of shock. There stood the one child in the orphanage she would never have guessed to be her little phantom. Before her stood the child considered by many of the nuns to be their worst nightmare, the child most likely to be branded as the most mischievous boy in the Saint Anthony's Home for Boys.

Nicholas stood looking at her with teary eyes as he put out his shaky little hands. His little lips started to quiver as he waited for the beating he was sure would follow his discovery. When Sister Clara saw him put out his hands she was puzzled until she realized that she had a ruler in her hand. She immediately threw it down and called Nicholas over to her. Sister Clara couldn't help but get teary-eyed herself. Kneeling down she took his battered little hands into her own as she cried softly. She wondered how such a small boy could bravely accept such barbaric punishment.

Sister Clara was overwhelmed with emotion. She hoped she could give music lessons to this child who was so determined to play the piano that he overcame his fear of punishment to enjoy a few stolen moments of music. Anyone this determined deserved all the help he could get. But for now, Sister Clara could not stop herself from crying as she held Nicholas's cold shaking hands up to her warm face. She was trying to show this scared little boy some affection, hoping it would ease his frightened feelings.

This situation puzzled Nicholas. This was not what usually happened when he got into trouble but right now, he gladly accepted her strange behavior. Nicholas was still expecting punishment from Sister Clara, but she could only shake her head in disbelief at this child. He was always the boy in trouble, she had never suspected he had such an interest in playing the piano. Who would have guessed he had such talent? As this thought came into her mind she realized that there had been signs that had been ignored. Nicholas had displayed an interest in music as he played the harmonica.

She suddenly remembered that the Sunday she had played the piano for her group of boys was the same day that Nicholas had been sick. Such a strange coincidence in the events of life. Sister Clara was sad when she thought about the effort that Nicholas had to go through to break the rules so he could play the piano.

In the seconds it took for these thoughts to race through Sister Clara's mind, Nicholas, being so naïve, believed she was crying because he had made her so angry that she didn't know what to do with him. He looked at Sister Clara with his sad brown eyes and said softly, "I'm sorry Sister."

As Sister Clara came to her senses she said. "Nicholas, I want you to go back to your group. Do you know where you are supposed to be now? I will talk to you later."

"Yes Sister," answered Nicholas before he turned to run out of Sister Clara's sight.

"Oh Lord," prayed Sister Clara, "Please forgive me for not reporting this situation to my superior. But I couldn't bare it if I knew Nicholas received another beating. Especially now that I know how brave he is and how much he loves music. I will do my best to keep Nicholas from getting hit with the ruler again. He has wonderful hands. It is possible that someday he could be one of the world's great pianists. I will give my time to him and teach this child everything I know about music. I will also teach him the manners that I learned at his age so that he will be accepted as a classical pianist. I have the deepest feeling about this child. I can't explain what draws me to him even beyond his gifted talent. Was this special feeling secretly behind my obsession to find this mysterious young man? There is something wonderful and powerful in his music."

The following day when Sister Clara had some free time, she took Nicholas aside to have her talk with him. She told him that she wanted to teach him how to play the piano the proper way. She was careful not to embarrass him by criticizing his way of playing, but she explained to him the advantage of learning to read music versus his way of replaying what he heard. Sister Clara told Nicholas that there would have to be a tradeoff in this partnership. She would give him piano lessons, but in exchange he must try to stay out of trouble as much as possible.

Nicholas readily agreed to this bargain, but Sister Clara knew it was impossible for him to change so quickly. She doubted that he could stay completely out of trouble, but at least she hoped she could get him to reduce the number of occasions. From this day on, Sister Clara appointed herself to be the Guardian Angel that Nicholas so desperately needed. She knew it would be a hard and rough road ahead, but she was looking forward to it. She still had a strong feeling that Nicholas would someday be a great pianist.

Nicholas wasted no time in starting his lessons with Sister Clara. She included small hidden lessons on his manners, working also on the appearance of his hands. She urged him not to bite his fingernails. She rubbed his hands with medicated lotion and told him that good healthy hands were of great importance in playing the piano. Nicholas was as excited to receive the piano lessons as Sister Clara was to give the lessons. He had never really paid much attention to Sister Clara before but now he saw her as a loving and caring person. Sister Clara had always been a gentle, soft-spoken patient nun.

2

Nicholas was six years old when Sister Clara started giving him piano lessons. He had a lesson everyday except Sunday. It was more difficult to learn to read notes then it was to play by ear but the challenge did not discourage him. His lessons continued for years and Nicholas progressed rapidly due to Sister Clara's patience and love. Now he realized how much better music sounded and how much easier it was to play music because he knew how to read the written notes. Only one year remained before Nicholas passed the age limit of the orphanage and he would have to leave the home.

One day, Sister Clara approached Nicholas to tell him that she was going on vacation for a week to visit her mother and father. When she returned, they would continue with his lessons. She left Nicholas with instructions on the lessons he was to practice while she was away.

Through the years of being together, Sister Clara and Nicholas had formed a close bond. Sister Clara had been taught that a nun should never get close or attached to anyone but God. This was to ensure that performance and duties were not influenced by human loyalties. Sister Clara realized that she must work hard to serve God and help one of His creations (Nicholas) at the same time.

She believed that God had given Nicholas a special talent and placed her in a position to help him to develop his gift. This was the only time that Sister Clara had gone against the rules.

Nicholas had become the son that Sister Clara never had and Sister Clara had become the mother that Nicholas never knew. The two had never been apart before and while Sister Clara was away, they both realized that they missed each other. Nicholas was able to stay out of trouble while his Guardian Angel was away. He was just too busy with his lessons to find time to get into trouble. This once mischievous little boy was reaching the age of maturity. When Sister Clara returned from her visit, they resumed both the lessons and their togetherness.

Since Sister Clara and Nicholas had been working together, Nicholas had lost most of his shyness. He smiled readily and they both were always laughing for one reason or another. At Sister Clara's insistence, Nicholas had also lost the habit of biting his fingernails.

The future was looking bright for Nicholas. He had truly come a long way from the frightened six-year-old little boy he was when Sister Clara first began his lessons. It was almost as if a miracle had been performed by a nun there at the Saint Anthony's Home for Boys. She had been teaching Nicholas everything that she had learned and as a result, Nicholas had become a great pianist. But Sister Clara was not satisfied, she felt he needed more lessons. She wanted desperately for Nicholas to go to college and earn his Master's degree in piano music.

The time for Nicholas to leave the orphanage had arrived. He didn't like the idea of having to part from Sister Clara. Generally, when the boys grew to old for the orphanage, they were transferred to a Boy's Ranch until they reached the age of 21. Sister Clara, acting as a smart Guardian Angel, had planned ahead to the time of Nicholas' release. At the time of her visit with her parents the year prior to his release from the orphanage, she had a long and convincing discussion with them about Nicholas.

Before taking her vows to become a nun, her name had been Clara Angelica Fulton. She was the only child of Ben and Jane Fulton. As a child, her wealthy parents had given her everything she had wanted. Ben Fulton, her father, was a successful businessman who loved his daughter dearly. At six feet four inches he was a tall, slender man with a deep voice. There was now a sprinkle of white in the natural brown color of his mustache and in his receding hairline. Jane Fulton, Sister Clara's mother, was just above the average height for a woman at five feet eight inches. She was a slightly overweight, extremely charming woman. Years before, Jane Fulton had lost her voice as a result of cancer. Ben and Jane Fulton had been happily married for 30 years.

When Sister Clara had visited her parents a year prior, she had pleaded with them to take Nicholas into their home to sponsor him in college and allow him to live with them until he had earned his Master's degree in music. Her parents had not been crazy about the idea of having a strange young man living in their home. But the Fultons were very loving parents who agreed with the plan, for the sake of their only child. They felt that she had given up her freedom to become a nun. "One sacrifice deserves another," thought Mr. Fulton as he looked at his daughter.

Sister Clara truly deserved a set of wings as Nicholas' Guardian Angel. When she explained the plans for his future, he was ecstatic. He grabbed her to give her such a big hug that he almost knocked her to the ground. That is how it happened that Nicholas went to live with the Fultons to attend the same college that Clara Angelica Fulton had attended.

Sister Clara had done her part to teach Nicholas everything she knew about the art of piano music. She had also spent some time teaching him socially correct mannerisms and the proper way of speaking the English language. What a stroke of luck it was for Nicholas, that he would be nurtured by all three Fultons. As Sister Clara and Nicholas said their farewells, tears fell heavily from them both.

"Write to me, Nicholas. Let me know about everything that happens with you," Sister Clara said as she hugged Nicholas. When she started to let go Nicholas did not want to end the embrace. He held on to Sister Clara tightly and she returned the hug again. This scene was no different than if a son was leaving his mother. As the taxi drove away, Nicholas looked back to Sister Clara from the rear window of the taxicab, still teary-eyed, gazing until he could no longer see her. Sister Clara stood waving until the cab disappeared from view. As the taxicab headed to the airport, Nicholas started thinking about how much he was going to miss Sister Clara. He would also miss the orphanage because it had been the only home Nicholas had ever known.

A few days after his arrival, Mr. Fulton drove Nicholas to the college to register for his classes. School would not begin for another week and Nicholas could hardly contain his excitement. He thought frequently about Sister Clara. He knew that she had made it possible for him to be with her parents for this great adventure. Without the love and kindness of all three

Fultons, Nicholas would be at the Boy's Ranch, probably getting into trouble.

When Nicholas registered at the college for his classes, he also signed up for courses in sign language. He wanted to be able to communicate with Mrs. Fulton. As time went on, Nicholas did write to Sister Clara at least once a month. Ben and Jane Fulton grew really fond of Nicholas. Their daughter's idea for Nicholas to live with them had the extra benefit that she came to visit more frequently.

• • •

After years of schooling only a few months remained before Nicholas graduated with high honors. He had become a fantastic pianist. When he received his Master's degree in music, he would finish the course started years before by Sister Clara. Nicholas had also turned out to be a good-looking young man. He had a slender body with black shoulder length hair. His complexion was olive toned and he had hazel brown eyes that drew the attention of many young ladies. While Ben and Jane Fulton were excited about Nicholas's graduation, Sister Clara was the one who was the most thrilled. She thought back to the mischievous little boy with the harmonica in his back pocket. The other nuns had thought of him as the terror of Saint Anthony's Home for Boys. Today he was tall, handsome and very well mannered. No one who had known Nicholas when he was a child in the orphanage would have believed that he would turn out like this.

"Thank you Lord, for helping me all these years and blessing me with the strength to help an abandoned child to become a wonderful young adult. Thank you for giving me parents that are loving and caring. Thank you especially for Nicholas. He has brightened up my life. Now I know how a mother feels about her own child even without giving birth. If nothing else great ever happens for the rest of my life, I will forever be grateful for having this chance, Amen." Sister Clara offered this prayer on graduation day as she joined her parents in attending the ceremony. She had taken a leave of absence from the orphanage for the occasion.

A few days after the graduation, Sister Clara was scheduled to return to the orphanage. Nicholas was truly a changed young man. On his diploma he had shortened his name to Nick. When Sister Clara looked at the certificate and noticed what he had done she remarked, "You will always be Nicholas to me," as tears rolled down her cheeks. "After hearing you play the piano for us the other evening, I am glad that you are the one who finished what I started. Even when you were little, I felt that with your natural talent you would benefit from it more than I would have." After saying good-bye to her parents she took her leave.

A few weeks after the graduation Ben and Jane Fulton departed for a vacation in Paris. Sadly, they did not make it to their destination. The plane crashed in the ocean and it was reported that there were no survivors. The tragic news was almost as devastating to Nick, who had grown to love them, as it was to Sister Clara. At the simple funeral, Nick delivered a eulogy that put many into tears.

Nick felt especially guilty because the Fultons had given him so much, opening their arms to a total stranger and now he would never have a chance to repay them. His farewell gift was to give a speech of praise to thank them dearly for being so caring.

A month after the funeral Sister Clara had time to empty the house and list it with a real estate broker for sale. She had met with her father's legal counsel who would take care of the probate of the estate. Sister Clara made provisions to give half of her inheritance to Nick and the other half donated to the Saint Anthony's Home for Boys. She knew that the time had come for Nick to live on his own.

"So what do you plan on doing now, Nicholas?" Sister Clara asked with concern.

His reply was, "Right now I just need a few weeks by myself to think things out. I know I want to become the great pianist you believe I can be. I want you to be proud of the work and trust you have placed in me."

They had a long talk; Sister Clara was still trying to be the Guardian Angel she had become years ago for Nick. She realized that when Nick left to be on his own, she would no longer be able to watch over him.

"I know you're a mature young man now and I am so proud of the person you have become but you will always be my little Nicholas. Oh, please be careful." At last, they parted Sister Clara returned to the orphanage and Nick headed to Philadelphia.

Nick did not want to reside in an oversized city like New York even though the opportunities were greater there. He knew that if Philadelphia did not offer the openings he was looking for he could try another city. So Nick spent a few weeks in Philadelphia looking around the city. After only one month, he was employed to play with a small orchestra. His Master's degree in music would help to open many doors but Nick had a plan and the small orchestra would do for a start.

During his first six months, Nick developed the habit of joining some of the other musicians from the orchestra at a local tavern to have several drinks after each concert. When his companions had a few drinks, they each left for home but Nick always stayed behind for more. Soon Nick found that he was unable to stop drinking when his friends stopped for the evening. He eventually began to stay until the tavern closed at 2 a.m.

As his drinking became worse, he began to miss work. The manager of the orchestra gave Nick many warnings but after he ignored them all, Nick was dismissed. Even though he was a fantastic pianist, he was not reliable. The loss of his job did not seem to bother Nick. His friends tried to get him to stop drinking but Nick unfortunately had become an alcoholic. His reaction to alcohol was so strong that in a short time, he could not control his drinking. His fellow musicians urged him to seek help in a medical facility for alcoholics. They knew that Nick would not be able to stop by himself and would eventually drink himself into trouble.

The loss of his job was the first step down the path to trouble. But the only thing that mattered to Nick was where his next drink would come from. Everything else was of no concern to him. As his acquaintances became aware of his problem drinking, they worried about his future. He was young and in trouble. What was going to become of his dream to be a great pianist? Was this the end of a promising future?

Sister Clara was not aware of what was happening to Nick. She had been having a difficult time working through her grief following the death of her parents. She spent more time in prayer and sought the counsel of the church. She thought that Nick was spending his time working on his own feeling of grief.

Nick found himself drinking until he could not remember what he did nor how he managed to return to his own apartment each night. He tried to stop but the craving was too overpowering and instead, he spent more time drinking. He slowly lost his self-respect and the respect of his friends. Alcohol had no preference.

If Sister Clara had known what was happening to Nick, she would probably have had a breakdown. Back at Saint Anthony's, she was worried because she had not received a letter from Nick. All of the letters that she had written to Nick recently had been returned, stamped, "MOVED WITH NO FORWARDING ADDRESS," across the front of the envelope. Nick had been evicted from his apartment because he could not pay the rent. Nick drank away all of his money.

Soon, the streets of Philadelphia were home for Nick. Sister Clara spent many sleepless nights in prayer as she waited to hear from him. She worried about his health and his safety. Nick lived or more truthfully, survived on the streets of Philadelphia for two years. He would not have been recognized by anyone who had known him before. One day, Nick was sitting on a park bench suffering with the shakes caused by alcohol withdrawal. He needed a drink so desperately that he stole a woman's purse and was caught a block from where the purse was snatched. Nick was sentenced to two years in prison by the judge. His term could be reduced to one year with good behavior.

Nick attended Alcoholics Anonymous meetings while he was in prison and after several months, he began to feel better. He could control his craving for alcohol. The sentence had been a blessing in disguise. As time passed, he became friendly with his cellmate, Mark. Before prison Mark had been a circus clown. As cellmates, they watched out for each other.

Nick and Mark both decided to join with the other inmates in the weekly performance put on as entertainment for their fellow inmates. After spending two years living on the streets, Nick could still play the piano extremely well, as if he had never been away from the piano. But Nick knew that he would have to spend a lot of time practicing to get his badly disfigured fingers to respond correctly to his commands.

In the meantime, he was able to play the piano while Mark performed a comedy skit as a clown. Mark dressed in a spectacular looking outfit to disguise himself as a hobo. Nick found this disguise intriguing. Mark did not overly apply the makeup to his face like most clowns. He put on only enough to hide his face so no one would be able to recognize who he was behind the makeup.

One day Nick asked Mark to teach him about the art of makeup and how to make people laugh. "Putting on makeup is simple, once you get the hang of it," Mark explained to Nick. "As for acting, you will be surprised to find that once your mask of makeup is on, you will feel like a different person. You will find that you throw away all shyness and it is like a magic spell has been cast over you. It is amazingly easy to act the part of the character you have designed the mask to portray. It's amazing what being behind a mask can make you do to lighten up someone's face. And when you see smiles and hear the laughter, then nothing holds you back from performing to the utmost."

As time passed, Nick received an education from Mark about the professional application of makeup. He also had lessons on how to perform a comic routine that was funny enough to make people laugh. As the months passed, Nick learned everything Mark had to offer.

One evening when Nick found himself alone, he began to think of Sister Clara. Nick felt that he had failed her, even though she knew nothing of his circumstances. So many years had passed since he had contacted her, she must wonder if he was still alive. The guilt began to weigh heavily on his conscience. He decided to write a letter to Sister Clara to explain everything that had happened and ask her for forgiveness.

So Nick addressed his letter to Saint Anthony's Home for Boys and hoped that she would be happy to hear from him. The return address on the envelope frightened Sister Clara but she was eager to read this letter from Nick. Tears fell down her face as she read through the entire letter. When she was finished, she stopped for a therapeutic crying session. She had waited a long time to hear from Nick and the agony of his battle with alcoholism caused her heart to break. Sister Clara had an uncle who was alcoholic so she was well acquainted with this disease. She could tell from the way that Nick had written his letter that she needed to take a trip to visit him. Taking a leave of absence, she headed for Philadelphia.

She had called ahead to find out the schedule of visiting hours. It was Saturday afternoon and Nick was exercising his fingers on an upright piano. He had been given special privileges from the guards because they knew that he was a professional pianist. They also knew what Nick had been through, the look of his hands and fingers gave evidence of his hard life. He needed as much practice as he could get to bring himself back to the level were he was when he graduated.

While Nick was practicing on the piano, a guard came to tell him that he had a visitor waiting to see him. After his initial surprise, he could think of only one person who would visit him in prison. That person could only be Sister Clara.

Nick was excited but at the same time, he was scared and embarrassed to face her. As a child, Nick had always accepted the punishment for his crimes but he was as nervous now as he was when he was six years old and had been found playing the piano in an abandoned classroom. A nun was waiting in the visiting room, dressed in her familiar habit, and whose beautiful face Nick was delighted to see.

This prison facility allowed visitors to touch the prisoners they were visiting. Under the close observation of the guards, Nick embraced Sister Clara. They would have spent their entire visit holding each other but the rules would not permit extended contact. The guards made an exception to the brief time period allowed because they recognized the social distinction between a nun and a female visitor.

Sister Clara and Nick were glad to see each other. They had much to discuss to catch up on the years without communication between them. At the end of the visit, Sister Clara assured Nick that she would be back the next day. She also mentioned that she would be going into the hospital for minor surgery but that he should not worry about her.

Sister Clara promised Nick that when his prison term was finished, she would send him a plane ticket to fly back home to Albuquerque. When Sister Clara left the prison, Nick felt as homesick as he did the first time he left the boy's home. But he also felt as if a weight had been removed from his shoulders. That night, Nick got down on his knees to say a long prayer of thanksgiving for his Guardian Angel, Sister Clara.

A month before Nick's prison term was over, a large envelope arrived at the prison, addressed to him. Sister Jessica at the Saint Anthony's Boys Home had enclosed two letters inside the large envelope. One letter was labeled on the front, "Please read first." It was from Sister Jessica. It read, "Dear Nicholas. I'm sorry that I must be the bearer of bad news. Sister Clara's surgery was not the minor operation that she probably mentioned to you. She confided to me that she had not wanted you to worry.

I'm sorry to say that Sister Clara passed away on the operating table Friday afternoon. We at the Saint Anthony's Home for Boys will truly miss her. She had left word with me that if by chance something were to go wrong with the operation, I should get in touch with you to let you know of the situation."

"Oh Sister Clara," whispered Nick, as tears ran down his anguished face. He did not read the letter from Sister Clara until the shock and disbelief had begun to ease. Then he peeked at the letter. The front of the envelope read, "To my dearest Nicholas." Nick opened the envelope slowly, somewhat afraid to read her letter.

The letter began, "My dearest Nicholas. The only reason you will be reading this letter is if something has gone wrong with the operation. I'm truly sorry I have had to leave you, especially now when you need me the most. But the Lord has called me for His own reasons. Now that I am gone, you will need to find the strength within yourself to take control of your life again. I have always had faith in you. Now that you are alone, don't let yourself down. Now you only have God to rely on."

As Nick continued to read the long letter, he had to pause a few times just to wipe the tears from his eyes. There was a postscript at the bottom of the letter. "P.S. I will work on the Lord so that I may continue to be your Guardian Angel." Nick broke down, crying uncontrollably until he could cry no more. He realized at that moment that he was truly alone in this world.

"What do I do now?" he thought. "I can't even begin to think straight at this moment. I need time to mourn." Nick only wanted to be left alone so he kept to himself for several days. Understanding his grief, Mark gave Nick space and the time he needed to mourn.

One night while Nick was lying in bed and thinking of the past, present and future, he whispered silently to himself, "I want to change my ways to become a better man. I truly want to leave the horror of the past behind me. I am ready to deal with the present and I will work toward building a future that would make Sister Clara proud of me." Then sleep overcame him.

The last month in prison was harder on Nick than the previous eleven months. He was biding time, counting the days, waiting for his release date. He was both excited and frightened. During his stay in prison, he had made many friends, including some of the guards. Nick had even grown accustomed to the prison life. The conditions inside the prison were many times better than the conditions he had faced living on the street. Now he was afraid of facing the outside world again. Nick viewed his return outside as a test of endurance. He knew that he was stronger than before he was sent to prison because now, he was facing the outside world with a sober mind. But Nick questioned himself, "Will I be able to pass a bar or liquor store? Can I fight the urge to stop for a drink or buy a bottle of the devil's brew?"

Nick planed to use the steps taught to him at Alcoholics Anonymous. He knew that it only took the first drink to go back on the road to hell. The thoughts of drinking again sent cold chills down his back and caused the hairs in the back of his neck to stand up. He didn't ever want to be in that kind of situation again. To avoid any problems, Nick had to find an AA facility so that he could attend the meetings and remain a sober man.

After a year in prison without any alcohol in his system, Nick was looking more like the man who had lived with the Fultons. However, there were some changes to his body from his two years of living on the streets. Nick was anxious to spend more time playing the piano. He appreciated the amount of time he was allowed practice while in prison. The upright piano he used had been donated to the prison but it was kept under lock and key and only limited access was allowed. It could be used only under the supervision of the guards so that none of the prisoners could remove any parts for use to make a weapon.

His first priority was to find a job. The day of his release, Mark had a long talk with Nick, coaching him like an older brother, giving Nick his opinions and suggestions about precautions to use while out on the streets.

Mark was short and slightly overweight. He had never been married. He was sentenced to 15 years in prison for killing a man in a hit and run accident while driving intoxicated. Mark was an alcoholic who now had a long time to sober up in prison. In his life before the accident, he had worked as a circus clown.

The glorious day finally arrived for Nick to walk outside as a free man. The outside air felt so much cleaner than the air behind the prison walls. Nick took a deep breath and looked around at the world past the prison gates.

The Corrections Department had arranged for a place for Nick to board after his release. He could stay there until he was able to find a job and another place of his choice to live. The Corrections Department usually had a job lined up also for released prisoners. But Nick wanted to find work for himself for personal reasons.

The morning following his release Nick started roaming the streets of Philadelphia. His first step was to go back to the locations where he had spent 2 years of agony on the streets. He noticed that someone else had taken his place and shook his head in sorrow. Nick was happy that now he was only an observer. He bowed his head for a minute to say, "Thank you, Lord, for giving me another chance in life."

Then Nick began to search for a job and a new place to stay. His limited funds still offered enough money to rent a better apartment than the place the Corrections Department had arranged. While Nick was roaming the streets, he met a few homeless people and the memories of his life just before prison return made him feel uneasy. "Never again, never again," whispered Nick.

Even though he had a limited amount of money, he offered some help to these homeless people. He knew what it was like to walk in their shoes, so he was compelled to give them any money he could spare. Now, Nick was on the other side of the fence, looking at the homeless the same way as others had looked at him when he was living on the streets. He knew that he must be realistic, he couldn't give all of his money away to the homeless. He couldn't take care of them and himself as well

After two days of job hunting, luck came knocking on Nick's door. Nick accepted a job in a music store as a salesperson. Prior to his release from prison, with the help of the correctional center, Nick had put together a resume with photocopies of his college certificate and Master's degree. He had sent for the information because he knew he would need it for his job interviews. While in prison, Nick had learned to talk to the other prisoners and work his way into their minds. It was a matter of survival to avoid being taken advantage of by other inmates.

So Nick learned how to talk his way out of a bad situation and what to say in order to get along with everyone in the prison facility, even if it meant lying through his teeth. Of course there were a few exceptions. There were some people you just could not get along with no matter how hard you tried. That was just Nature's way. You either liked someone or you didn't. Having to deal with a variety of personalities in prison had given Nick some preparation for his new job.

Because of Nick's education his specialty would be the piano. After a few months with his new job, Nick was doing exceptionally well. He had found a very nice, inexpensive apartment and had purchased a fairly new console piano. He spent all of his free time practicing on the piano. Every now and then, Sister Clara would pop into Nick's mind, usually when he was playing one of her favorite selections on the piano. It seemed to Nick as if she was trying to tell him something. Nick stopped playing the piano and whispered softly, "I have not forgotten you, Sister Clara," and then he proceeded with his exercise on the piano.

3

Nick had made many new friends at work and at his apartment complex. The tenants on his floor who had heard him practice on the piano, complimented him on his playing. There was a young woman named Teresa, about Nick's age, who had taken a special interest in him. Teresa had taken some piano lessons while in high school. One day she asked Nick if he would give her piano lessons. (This was her way of spending time with him to get to know Nick better.) Nick responded by saying that he would be glad to teach her to play the piano, but he didn't know how long he would be able to continue the lessons.

Teresa was five feet six inches tall and she weighed around 130 pounds. She had blue eyes, with shoulder-length light brown hair, but the feature Nick found the most attractive was her smile. It was the most beautiful smile he had ever seen on a woman. He was intrigued with the smile that seemed familiar. After thinking about her smile he realized that it reminded him of the smile Elvis Presley had made famous, a little lip curl smile which gave way to Teresa's deep dimples. He thought of it as her "Special Smile."

Nick looked forward to seeing Teresa's special smile every time he met her. Nick didn't intend to become seriously involved with her. He didn't want anyone or anything to interfere with his plans for success. Getting involved with Teresa was not in his schedule, even though he was strongly attracted to her. Teresa began her piano lessons with Nick. He didn't have the heart to charge her. After all, the lessons he had received from Sister Clara had been given freely.

As time passed, Teresa realized that she was falling in love with Nick. She did not want him to know about her feelings because she was afraid he would respond with a rejection. She didn't think that Nick returned her affection so she kept her silence, satisfied to be with him during her lessons. She patiently looked for any sign or opening to get into his heart.

Teresa has had a difficult time struggling with several jobs to support herself as she went through college. She took only the necessary courses that were required to graduate with a degree in Library Science. She did add one extra class, sign language, to help her communicate with people who had a speaking or hearing impairment.

Teresa could read for hours. She was interested in just about any subject. She grew up in a small family with one brother and one sister. Now she seldom saw her siblings because both her parents were deceased and they no longer had a central meeting place. Teresa had become well adjusted to living by herself.

One day at work, a year after his release from prison, Nick overheard a co-worker named Sam discussing a problem with another co-worker named Jake. Sam was telling Jake that he had asked a friend who was a professional pianist to perform at his daughter's high school talent show in two weeks time. But now the friend had called Sam to say that he was unable to come to the program. Sam was frantic because schedules had already been printed with the names of those performing in the show. And now, because of a scheduling conflict, the pianist had cancelled his performance at the high school.

"This is a disaster!" Sam screamed. "How could he do this? My Jeanie is going to be devastated." He was working himself into a rage. Sam's daughter wanted to show off by getting this well-known musician to perform at her school. She was hoping to boost her popularity by arranging a special performance by a professional pianist. Jeanie was the student coordinator of the talent show; it was her responsibility to schedule each artist, hoping to insure that the evening would be a success.

"I just don't know how I'm going tell her. This will be a tragedy for her." Sam was a good father and husband; he would do just about anything for his family. He was always spoiling his only child, Jeanie. Anything Jeanie wanted, within reason, Jeanie received. Sam spent the rest of that day agonizing about how he was going to break the bad news to her. Sam was worthless at work and didn't make any sales that day. Nick could see his frustration.

At the end of the day Nick approached him. "Sam," he began, "I heard you discussing a problem earlier today about a pianist canceling out of your daughter's talent show. I'm really sorry to hear about that." Nick had speculated about this all day, his sympathy was with his friend who was in trouble, but he also wondered if this could be his first opportunity to start performing. He decided to get his feet wet.

"Sam, I would like to buy you a cup of coffee," Nick offered.

Sam looked at him with a question on his face, but responded; "I'm not in the mood for coffee right now, but thanks for asking. I've got to go home and break the bad news to Jeanie."

Nick was trying to persuade him. "If you come with me to the café around the corner and let me buy you coffee, I might be able to solve your problem. You won't have to go home and upset Jeanie."

Sam looked at Nick as if he thought that Nick had lost his mind. "Solve my problem?" muttered Sam.

"Yes that's right," replied Nick. "But I would like to discuss this with you over a cup of coffee."

Sam still looked puzzled saying, "Well alright, it should be interesting to see how you are going to solve my problem."

"You won't regret this Sam," Nick said with a confident gesture.

They walked around the corner to the café where Nick was known by all of the employees. Rather than cook for only himself Nick ate all his meals here. He was greeted by one of the waitresses, Deanna, as they entered the café.

"One strong black coffee for Nick," she wrote. Deanna already knew that was what Nick ordered first when he came in. "And what can I get for your friend, Nick?" she asked.

"Oh I'll have the same," Sam told her.

Deanna turned around to face the opposite direction with such a sharp spin that her dress flared up slightly. She gave Nick a smile followed by a wink as she headed back to get the coffee. As they waited for the coffee to arrive, Nick looked out the window of the café for a brief moment and spotted a homeless person going through the trashcan sitting outside in front of the café.

He excused himself he got up and went to ask Deanna to bag a half dozen doughnuts and a large coffee to go. Without any questions asked she gave Nick the bag of doughnuts and coffee.

Nick told Deanna, "I'll be right back, just add these to my bill," then he proceeded to walk outside to present the homeless man with the treats.

Sam wondered what would cause a man like Nick to do this? He thought it was nice but dismissed it from his mind. When Nick returned to the café after spending about five minutes talking to the man outside, Sam wondered what they could have been talking about that seemed so interesting to Nick. "Oh well, it doesn't really matter," he thought with a shrug. "I have more important problems to worry about than to think about that conversation."

Once Nick was settled back into his seat Sam turned to ask, "How do you think you can help me solve my problem?'

"Oh yes," said Nick, "When I approached you in the store about your problem, it was because I realized that I can get a musician to perform at you daughter's high school talent show."

Sam still had a puzzled look on his face. He was wondering where could Nick find a professional pianist to take the place of the one he had scheduled for the school's show. Sam took a sip of his coffee and then cleared his throat. "Who is the pianist that you think will perform for the school?" Sam questioned Nick. "Are you aware that no one performing at the school will be paid for their appearance? I just wanted to be certain you understood this when you speak to this musician."

"I do understand there is no payment for this program, Sam. Charlee is the name of this pianist I have in mind," answered Nick.

Sam thought this over and replied, "Charlee... Charlee... Nope, I've never heard of a pianist by the name of Charlee."

"Well," said Nick, "this pianist isn't well known, but he is very talented."

"I don't know," replied Sam, "You see, Nick, I know the quality of performance we would have from the professional pianist that was going to perform for us. The only reason he agreed was because he owes me a favor. He was going to return the favor by playing in my daughter's show. I've never heard of a pianist named "Charlee". I don't know if he can perform to the level of my expectations. I don't want to take the chance of embarrassing my daughter in front of her friends. I need to meet with Charlee and have him audition for me. This way, I'll know if I want to ask him to perform for the school show."

"I'm afraid that's out of the question," said Nick. "You see, Charlee is mute and it would be hard to communicate with him unless you know sign language. There isn't enough time before the date of your daughter's program to have him schedule an audition." Nick needed a small miracle. He was wondering how he could convince Sam to agree.

"Look Sam," said Nick. "You have gotten to know me pretty well by now. Can you trust my judgement about this? I wouldn't try to help you if I didn't know what Charlee's performing abilities are. Trust me when I say that he is very good. Charlee probably is more talented than the pianist you had scheduled to perform."

"That is hard to believe," Sam replied. "What makes you believe that Charlee is better than the pianist I had scheduled to perform at my Jeanie's school?"

Nick was trying hard to convince Sam to accept his plan. "Trust me Sam, you just have to trust me. This pianist is truly outstanding," Nick stated with confidence.

"Nick, do you understand my concern," asked Sam. "I want someone very special to play in my daughter's talent show," he stated uneasily.

"Charlee can play any type of music you might want to hear. His repertoire includes selections of everything from classical to rock, with jazz and some honky tonk music as well. Now, that's a lot of talent," Nick said with a smile. He laughed at himself because he realized he was putting himself on a pedestal. "I've heard Charlee play many times and you can believe me when I say that Charlee is greater than you can ever imagine," Nick stated with authority.

"Why don't you think this over tonight and let me know in the morning if you want him to perform. I can't wait any longer than tomorrow night to contact him because the show is only two weeks away and he would need some time to prepare. When you are thinking about this just remember; right now you don't have anyone. This way you would have someone to perform, even if you've never heard of Charlee. Think of your daughter's feelings. I can guarantee that Charlee will not embarrass you or your daughter. It's your choice, Sam. This is my offer as a friend."

"I know you're just trying to help," said Sam. "I do appreciate your concern."

Just as Nick and Sam were finishing their coffee, there was a tap on the window that startled them both. When they turned to face the window they saw a smiling Teresa waving her hand. Nick felt as if she had brightened up his evening with the special smile that infatuated him. Teresa's nose was red from the cold

January temperature. Nick motioned for her to come inside and join them. She waved back with a gesture to indicate that she could not and then waved good-bye. Nick looked at Sam and said, "That's Teresa, my neighbor."

Nick noticed that Sam did not seem as worried now, as he had been all day. Sam appeared to be a lot calmer. Nick was anxious to return to his apartment to continue his practice on the piano.

The most important thing in Nick's life at this time was his music. The hours he spent in practice was like time spent in mental therapy. His existence before prison had been from one bottle to the next. Nothing else mattered except his next drink. His life now was so changed it was as if prison had been a time of re-birth. It was amazing how Nick's two lives were so different. He had become someone who cared for others feelings and had respect for himself and for humanity.

Nick's hands did not look as if they belonged to a pianist. His hands looked abused with many scars covering his crooked fingers. Teresa had noticed Nick's hands, but she had never made any comments about them. She was amazed that he could play such marvelous music with such unappealing hands. As Teresa began to fall in love with Nick she accepted the condition of his hands as she accepted everything else about him.

What she did not realize was that these hands were the result of his abused life. What the nuns had started in the orphanage before he met Sister Clara had been only a minor prelude to the damage from two years of living on the streets. His hands had been stepped on, bitten by stray dogs and cut many times by broken glass or the tops of open cans while going through garbage bins and cans. Some of the damage to his hands was from fights in his own defense.

Nick was not pleased by the looks of his hands, but could not change their appearance. He accepted the consequences for his past. Today his hands were precious to him. He knew that even as ugly as they were his hands performed to his every command, striking the keys to create some of the most beautiful music that could be played on the piano. Without feeling conceit, Nick was aware of his exceptional ability as a pianist. He considered it a talent that was his responsibility to share with others.

Sam took the last sip of his coffee, then turned to say, "Well, I need to go home. I'll let you know tomorrow."

Nick got up from his seat, shook hands with Sam and replied, "Sam everything is going to be OK. Sleep on your decision and let me know tomorrow." After Sam left the café, Nick remained sitting there, thinking about the best way to present Charlee.

Instead of planning for his performance, thoughts of Teresa entered his mind. It had taken Nick several months to realize that she was attracted to him. Her emotions had been revealed by the way she acted. As much as Teresa tried to keep her feelings bottled up, the bottle had a slight leak and some of her emotions had spilled out for him to see. Nick mistakenly believed that what she felt toward him was only an infatuation.

He had been careful to hide his attraction to her. It was hard not to care for a person as sweet and loving as Teresa. But Nick did not want to get involved in a relationship at this time. He needed all of his time to work out his career plan. Still thinking about Teresa, he remembered the last time he went to pay his rent. He always took time to sit and have coffee with the landlord. They always found something of interest to talk about.

This time, the landlord told him about what happened after Nick had moved into the building. He had been making rounds through the building to check the hall lights to see which fixtures had burnt out bulbs so that he could replace them the following day. "As I was walking toward your apartment, I noticed a young lady standing against the wall beside your door. She was another tenant who lives in this building. Because she wasn't a stranger I didn't worry about her being in the hallway."

"I asked her anyway if everything was OK. She whispered when she told me that everything was fine. Just at that moment, I heard you start to play the piano and I realized why she was there. All she wanted was to hear the beautiful music that you play on your piano. Anyway, I have seen her standing by your door several more times, as I have made my rounds every month. Now, when we see each other, all we do is wave so as not to disturb her concentration on your music. Many of the tenants on your floor tell me that they love listening to your music and ask me if I know whether you are a professional pianist. Some of the them say that they turn off the TV or radio just so they can listen to you play."

Nick was amazed by this story. He was even more curious about his silent fan. He asked the landlord if he could describe the young lady who was caught eavesdropping outside his door. "She is around five and one half feet tall, she has light brown hair that touches her shoulders and the prettiest deep blue eyes I have ever seen. You are lucky to have such a pretty admirer," said the landlord.

Nick knew right away that the young lady was Teresa. Nick didn't know that she had developed the habit of coming to his door in the evening just to listen to him practice. She could savor the pleasure his music without interrupting his concentration. Snapping out of his daydream Nick paid the bill and left the café for his apartment. He spent the evening in his usual manner, playing the piano.

The next day at work, Sam came to Nick and asked if Charlee could perform at his daughter's school. "Oh, yes," Nick excitedly replied. "I can arrange to have Charlee perform for you. I spoke to him last night. I wanted to alert him to the possibility that he might be needed." Sam asked Nick to meet him after work to discuss more of the details. This time Sam would be the one buying the coffee at the café.

Nick paused to look up, smile and whisper softly, "Oh Sister Clara, I'm excited and frightened. I could use the influence of your precious magical fingers, just in case mine decide to give out on me. It's been a long time since I have performed in front of an audience." Nick realized that he had just talked himself into his long awaited dream. There would be no turning back now. This was his chance to walk with his head held high.

Nick would have a chance to use several of his remarkable ideas for this performance. He wanted to make it unusual and exciting. All day long he could think of nothing but what he was about to do. This was something he had planned for a long time. When Nick and Sam went around the corner for coffee after work to discuss the talent show Sam wasted no time in getting his point across.

"Let me make myself clear on this," he said to Nick. "My daughter, Jeanie, asked me to choose the music for the other pianist to perform at the program. Even though I am not one of the coordinators, I'm just as involved with this program as my daughter is, on a voluntary basis. I have an obligation as a father to make sure that my part will go right for Jeanie's sake. So that's why you will have to work with me on this matter." Sam was not comfortable with the fact that he would not meet Charlee prior to the program. He realized he really had no choice in this matter, but to go along with Nick, cross his fingers and hope that everything went right.

"Here is the music I want Charlee to play," said Sam. Nick looked it over.

"Wow," Nick accidentally said out loud. Sam thought Nick was impressed with the list because of the great selection of music.

Unfortunately, Nick was thinking that this music would put all of the students to sleep. "This was not the kind of music I would play to a crowd of high school students. This list of music would be fine to play to an audience of adults." What he said to Sam was, "I will leave this up to Charlee."

"Hey Nick," Sam said, "I'm still a little worried about Charlee. I won't feel comfortable until I hear him play the piano. We are committed to his performance and there is no turning back, once I leave here. I just hope and pray that Charlee is as good as you say. I won't be able to interrupt him once he starts to play. My trust is in your hands."

"I will give you the details about the program's scheduling, the location, and any other important information three days before the program." replied Sam. "Oh, by the way, I told Jeanie last night about the change in pianist. She' s not crazy about it either, but she will cross her fingers and trust you."

As Sam was leaving for home Nick remembered one last observation to make to him, "You keep saying "he" every time you mention Charlee. I've never told you whether Charlee was male or female. Are you aware that you have done that?"

Sam opened his mouth, then paused as if wanting to say something, but he could not find the words. He then shook his head, turned around and continued to walk out the door. After Sam left the café Nick stayed at the table to think. He hoped that when he was finished performing at her school, that Jeanie would be the envy of all her peers. He planed to give Sam something to talk about for a whole week; enough time for everyone at work to get tired of hearing him.

Nick was filled with a feeling of confidence. He remembered a favorite saying that Sister Clara had when she was giving him piano lessons. She would say, "Nick, when you have confidence in yourself everything you do will be easier." Then he realized that he had only nine days to prepare himself for the beginning of his dreams. He thought to himself, "If I can't prepare myself in nine days, then this is not the career for me."

As planned, three days before the program Sam gave Nick the final instructions for Charlee. "Make sure that Charlee signs the roster that will be put out for all of the performers. The coordinators need to verify that each person they have scheduled has arrived. I'm assuming you will be there with Charlee that evening," stated Sam.

Nick smiled and said, "I wouldn't miss it for the world." He still had a smile on his face when Sam left. If Sam knew who Charlee really was, he wouldn't believe it. Nick wanted to remain anonymous from the character of Charlee for several reasons. He wanted to maintain a separate identity from Charlee and keep his own identity private. Nick wanted to be recognized and accepted by his friends only as himself. All he really wanted to do was play the piano and he would be happy to let Charlee get all the recognition.

Because Nick had chosen to portray Charlee as a hobo he was sending a message about homeless people. It was hidden behind the outfit that Charlee wore. If you opened your eyes you would be able to see that there were people out there who were very talented in many ways. It might also surprise you to know there were homeless people like Nick who were educated with a Master's degree earned in college. The message was don't underestimate the homeless. There was a reason for each and every one of them being where they were at the moment. Nick hoped that because he had walked in those shoes in the past that now Charlee would send a whole new meaning to everyone about homeless people.

Charlee would be covered from head to toe with a disguise. Nick planned for the outfit to be so effective that no one would be able to see the person beneath. As an added precaution, the costume was designed so that no one would know if the person in the outfit was male or female. This should keep everyone guessing and even choosing whom they thought fit the character. The possibility that Charlee might be a female was a tribute to Sister Clara. Nick had always felt that she was denied her opportunity for recognition because of her quiet life at the orphanage. She unselfishly passed all of her knowledge of music to Nick, as she forfeited all of her free time to lessons. Sister Clara's magical fingers would be honored through Charlee. When anyone heard Charlee play, a lot of Sister Clara's style would be represented. Nick sadly thought, "You could say that I inherited her magical fingers." But at this time Nick would be the only one to know this. So Charlee would be a character of two faces. Even the spelling of the name Charlee could be used for either male or female.

Nick truly was so gifted with the ability to play the piano that it came to him as naturally as breathing. He was able to complete his piano drills in a shorter time than had been required in college. The day arrived for the talent show and Nick called the music store to take the day off. When he did not make it to work that Friday Sam began to worry.

4

Nick needed a little more time to organize himself. After all, this was his first performance in front of a real audience. Playing in front of the prisoners had been just fun and games to Nick, but this evening was quite different. Another reason Nick did not go to work was because he knew Sam would be asking questions about Charlee all day long. Nick planned for Sam to be in total shock when he saw Charlee for the first time. He knew that after the performance started Sam would be impressed by Charlee.

The talent show started at 6:00 p.m. on Friday evening. All of the people that were to perform had signed the roster and been recognized by the stage manager except Charlee. The show was going well. They had Charlee scheduled as the last person to perform. There were ten short segments scheduled that evening. So the show was anticipated to end about 10:00 p.m.

The organizers were honored that the school board was attending the program. They needed to make a judgement on whether the evening programs were worth having after school hours. Their presence had been required, whether they want to be there or not. The audience seemed to be having a good time.

Backstage Jeanie approached Sam. They were waiting to meet Charlee. "Daddy" she said, "Where is this Charlee who is supposed to play tonight? I haven't seen him. In fact I don't even know who Charlee is. I'm getting a little nervous."

Sam replied, "I don't know where Charlee is, let's just be patient for a bit longer." Jeanie nervously turned to check the roster. Sam was pacing back and forth while mumbling, "I don't even have Nick's phone number. Oh yea," he remembered, "He doesn't have a phone." Sam kept repeating that Nick said he wouldn't miss this for the world. "I just hope he is true to his word. After all, he was the one who was responsible for this pianist. I hope they don't let us down. Maybe I shouldn't have agreed to this idea. It was stupid of me. I don't even know this Charlee." The more time Sam thought about this, the more nervous he became. Soon he had worked himself into a state of panic. He recalled that Nick said Charlee could play anything, now he worried that Nick's idea of music might not be what he wanted to hear. Sam had the idea that because he had worked in a music store for years that he was an expert on the subject.

"I'm going to feel pretty stupid and Jeanie will probably never speak to me again if this doesn't go well." This was important both to Sam and Jeanie. "All I can do right now," thought Sam, "is cross my fingers and pray."

"Daddy, Daddy" Jeanie's voice broke into Sam's worried thoughts. "Charlee is here. I know Charlee is here." Jeanie was almost shouting with excitement. "Charlee signed the roster."

Sam asked, "Well where is he?"

They both looked around but could not see anyone they thought resembled a pianist. Sam and Jeanie were looking for a person dressed in a tuxedo like so many concert pianists. But they could not see anyone who fit that description.

"Maybe Charlee stepped out for a minute," suggested Jeanie.

"Well, I'm going to walk around and see if I can spot this Charlee. I'll try the men's room first." Sam was so nervous that he had forgotten what Nick said about assuming that Charlee was a male. Jeanie, who was unaware of the question about whether Charlee was either male or female, was also busily looking for a male pianist named Charlee.

At one point when Sam was distracted with worry, he turned around abruptly and almost knocked down a character that looked like a hobo. Sam gave him a disgruntled look and muttered; "Do you mind watching where you're going?" Although the accidental contact was Sam's fault all of his worry had made him forget his manners. Charlee brushed off his jacket, Sam looked like a chicken running around with its head cut off, bumping into everything and everyone.

Nick chuckled because while Sam was frantically looking for Charlee he had just stepped all over him. But Sam was looking for the image he expected to see of Charlee. Nick would love to see Sam's face when Charlee appeared on stage for the first time.

After fifteen minutes, Sam met Jeanie again. "Honey," said Sam. "I haven't spotted Charlee yet."

"I haven't seen anyone that resembles a pianist either, Daddy," said Jeanie. "Maybe he forgot something and thinks that he still has time to go back and get it." Jeanie was showing her panic in her statement.

"I just don't know,' said Sam in an angry voice. "This is really frustrating. We'll just have to sit tight for a little while. There is still time before it's Charlee's turn to perform."

Sitting on the bleachers in the gym where the show was being held, the school board was taking notes and giving each other their opinions about the talent show. The high school principal, Mr. Harper was sitting with the school board.

When Sam read the announcer's list of music which would be performed by Charlee he realized that it was a different list from the original selections printed on the program schedule that was being handed to the audience as they entered the gym to see the talent show. Sam couldn't believe what he was reading. The printed schedule for tonight's program had been made up three weeks prior to the show's date. The name of the prior pianist that had been scheduled to perform was scratched out and Charlee's name was written in as a substitute. So the program the audience had been given had nothing written about Charlee.

Sam realized that Nick knew this and decided to make up his own list of music. The change in musical selections would emphasize the change in performers. Sam was furious; he wondered why Charlee had changed most of the selections he had chosen for him to play. "Who does Charlee think he was that he could just change things to suite himself? How dare he do this to me?" Sam thought.

Now Sam was more determined to find Charlee before it was his turn to perform. Sam decided to have Nick and Charlee paged over the intercom during the intermission. Sam was planning to have a talk with Charlee. He wondered where Nick was, after all, he was responsible for Charlee being on the program. If Sam could find Nick, he thought that they both could talk to Charlee about changing the music back to the previous list.

Sam mentioned his plan to Jeanie, "When this next performance is over, as soon as the intermission begins, have Nick and Charlee paged. I'll get to the bottom of this," snapped Sam.

"What's wrong, Daddy?" asked Jeanie.

"Oh nothing dear. I just need to talk to Nick and Charlee." Sam was trying not to let his daughter know about the change of music. Sam had not told her that he had scheduled Charlee unseen and had never heard him play. This contributed the largest part of Sams worries. The ironic coincidence was that both Sam and his daughter Jeanie had passed Charlee in the hallway numerous times and didn't even know it. But Charlee knew how many times he had been passed. He knew that they were looking for him dressed in a tuxedo.

He did not want to spoil Sam's shock when Charlee walked on stage. The principal, Mr. Harper, had come back-stage during the intermission to compliment everyone who had performed during the first half of the program. "Hi Sam," said Mr. Harper. "Great show were having. Have you enjoyed it?"

"Oh yea, great show," responded Sam.

"I thought I would congratulate all the people who have finished performing. I wanted to make sure I got back here in time before they leave. Well, I'd better go back to my seat," said Mr. Harper. "I have guests waiting for me to return."

As the program continued there were only two performers remaining before it would be time for Charlee to play. Now Sam had even more to worry about. Mr. Harper had explained to Sam earlier in the evening that the school board was paying an unexpected visit to observe the program. At this point they were pleased with the concept that having these evening programs would keep a lot of the kids off the streets on Friday nights. These programs would give the students a supervised activity to attend. That was the reason the principal, Mr. Harper, had started the program. It was his hope that it would influence the other schools in the district to do the same. That was provided that the school board gave its approval.

Sam went looking for his daughter to check if she had found Charlee. When Sam spotted her she was frantically looking around. She reminded him of a lost child who was looking for her parents in a crowd. "Have you spotted Charlee?" Sam asked Jeanie.

"No, Daddy. And the most frustrating part is that I don't even know what Charlee looks like." Sam and Jeanie were in such a state of panic that they did not even notice the suspicious looking character waiting to perform. If they had been calmer, they would have been able to determine by elimination that this character was Charlee, the final performer.

Sam asked Jeanie, "Didn't you ask to have Nick and Charlee paged?"

Jeanie answered, "Yes, I did ask but I never heard them broadcast it over the intercom. They must have forgotten with all the excitement."

"Oh well," said Sam. "Charlee has signed in. So he must be around here. We will just have to keep our fingers crossed and hope this comes out all right."

"Daddy, what's going on here. You've said the same thing twice. Is there something you are not telling me? What is it Daddy?" Jeanie was anxious for an answer.

"Honey, don't worry, I'll tell you later, but right now let's just find a place where we can watch our mysterious pianist perform." All of the performers scheduled before Charlee had finished. The long awaited moment had finally arrived for this newcomer of entertainment, "Charlee."

As the announcer read Charlee's prepared introductory a grand piano was rolled onto the front of the stage. This piano did not belong to the school. It had been provided on loan with the compliments of the music store where Sam worked. A marquee with the name of the music store was hung from the side of the piano.

"And now, ladies and gentlemen," shouted the announcer, "I give you Charlee." The anticipation built for Charlee to appear. When Nick had been in prison he had learned how to prepare the minds of his fellow inmates for his performance. This was the same type of situation; Nick was working to prepare the minds of the audience. This was to keep the audience focused directly on Charlee. The anticipation turned into a restless silence as everyone in the high school gym waited for the evening's final performer. But still, no one appeared. Complaints and mumbling began to come from the audience, as they all looked at each other with confusion.

Then from between the centerfolds of the stage curtains, popped out a head wearing mask of makeup and a hat. Sam was stretching his neck to get a glimpse of Charlee. With only his head showing, the audience began to applaud. This was an attractive face, it was not made to look like a clown from the circus. Charlee's head turned and looked to the left side of the stage and then turned and looked to the right side of the stage. When he appeared satisfied that both sides were clear of people, Charlee looked up suspiciously and then looked around again to make sure that no one was near. By this time, the audience was laughing. When Charlee finally walked out from behind the curtains the audience excitedly started to applaud followed by the sounds of whistles that echo in the gym. The pianist that was going to perform was standing on stage dressed as a hobo.

When Sam had a clear view of Charlee his eyes opened wide and his mouth dropped as he grabbed his chest. He thought he was going to have a heart attack. Jeanie had the same look of disbelief on her face. Sam was still trying to catch his breath as he mumbled a threat, "Nick and I are going to go round and round on this."

As Charlee stopped short of the center of the stage, he suspiciously turned to both sides, scratched his head and looked confused. The audience began to laugh. Charlee was about the most unique looking hobo that had ever been seen by this group. Nick was disguised from top to bottom. The mask of makeup he had on his face was superb, not overly done or heavy. Starting at the top with a shabby hat, he wore a patched brown jacket and white gloves, his pants were off-colored and patched. The total effect ended with shoes camouflaged with overlapping canvas rags tied around them. This was Charlee dressed up in his finest.

As Charlee walked to the front of the stage he put both hands up to his forehead to shield his eyes from the bright lights that were shining in his face so that he could get a better look at the audience. Charlee began looking high and low into the bleachers at the audience in a bit of confusion. The audience again broke into laughter. Charlee walked to the other side of the stage and did the same thing, getting more laughs.

When Nick had been leaving his apartment earlier that evening dressed in his costume he had been standing in the elevator when Teresa stepped in. He stood next to her as the elevator headed for the main floor of the building. He was encouraged when she did not immediately recognize him. He could feel Teresa's stare and when he turned in her direction he looked into her deep blue eyes. Then she surprised him with her special smile.

Nick was practically overcome with weakness with the thought that she had discovered who he was when she said, "Hi, my name is Teresa." Nick breathed a sigh of relief when he noticed that the lights from the ceiling of the elevator created a hazy halo effect above her head. He hoped that this was an omen of good luck.

His thoughts were interrupted when she asked him for his name. He automatically gave an answer in sign language that he was unable to speak. Teresa responded with a quick gesture of apology. Then she repeated her question in sign language. Nick was impressed with her knowledge of sign language when the elevator ride ended cutting short her conversation. As Nick walked toward the back door he signed, "Goodbye, hope to see you again." He was relieved that his disguise had passed this examination. He was now confident that his costume would pass Sam's inspection as well.

In the gymnasium, while the audience was laughing Charlee peered in their direction and gaped at them. Even without saying a word he had everyone laughing. Next Charlee began to do a few magic tricks. But of course, he failed every time. He was letting everyone quickly realize that he was NOT a magician and still he was getting several laughs with this act. So Charlee pretended to get fed up with the audience laughing at all of his failed magic tricks. Throwing both hands in the air, he started walking towards the stage curtains, shaking his head in disgust.

As Charlee headed toward the curtains, he passed to the left of a gorgeous looking grand piano. He gave it a slight glance as he passed, then his head turned forward again. He took a few more steps toward the curtains then. Then, as if he hadn't gotten the full effect of looking at this grand instrument, his head turned back to the piano. This time Charlee came to a screeching halt.

Charlee walked backward toward the piano. He stopped and stared at the piano sitting all by itself. He gazed at it in wonder as he scratched the back of his head. Then, Charlee started to look around in a sly manner. He looked behind himself, then to the sides. Then stretching his neck, he looked over the top of the piano to make sure no one else was around. He turned his focus to the piano keys and with one finger he played an offbeat tune.

The sound of the instrument created a tense anticipation in the audience. Charlee stopped again and after checking around to be sure that no one was close, he pulled the bench away to sit in front of the piano. He had to stand up several times to make himself comfortable, even turning the bench around as if that would make a difference. Then, he raised his hands slowly, holding them about a foot above the keyboard in preparation for a sudden impact.

Suddenly without warning, Charlee dropped his hands, stared at them and then started cracking his knuckles. You could feel the anticipation but at the same time, everyone was laughing at the knuckle cracking. Charlee shook both hands vigorously, as if trying to get the blood circulating through the fingers while at the same time, moving his head from side to side like a boxer trying to loosen up before a fight. The audience loved this preparation. Charlee pushed the bench back even further from under the piano. He stood up next to the grand piano, holding onto it with one hand he started doing knee bends. By now the audience was roaring with laughter. Charlee got down on the stage floor and did a few push-ups and finished the exercise with side-to-side body twists as if this exercise was a big help in performing. The laughter from the audience was getting louder.

The audience was so loud that Charlee stopped and peered at them, making a gesture as if to say, "What are you all laughing about. I'm just doing my exercises." He threw up both hands in the air, gesturing to the audience… "Phooey!" and walked back to the piano. Then Charlee sat down at the piano again, raised his hands and with a sudden impact, came down on the keys. He abruptly stood up, stepped away from the bench, gave a bow to the audience indicating the end of the performance and turned towards the stage curtains. He went behind the curtains leaving the audience in total wonder.

Just as fast as Charlee left the stage, he came flying back as if he was being thrown back from behind the stage curtains. He barely kept his balance to avoid falling down on the stage floor. Charlee now had the audience in tears of laughter. He looked at the audience for a second or two, just watching them laugh. When Charlee had spent enough time staring at them, he gestured to the audience to ask if they would still like for him to play for them. The audience again started to applaud and whistle so Charlee headed back to the piano.

Charlee then seemed to notice the outfit he was wearing. He looked at the jacket, pants and shoes. First Charlee removed the jacket, shaking his head in disbelief at this ridiculous outfit. He turned the jacket inside out to reveal a handsome black tailored coat. Then, Charlee took off his hat which was camouflaged with a thin piece of cloth, making the hat look extremely used. Charlee pulled down this piece of camouflaged cloth from the top part of the hat and tucked it inside the hat, making it now appear quite distinguished. The shoes were also camouflaged with overlapping canvas, making them look worn. Charlee pulled off the canvas which had been held on by Velcro. Now the shoes looked stylish. Charlee looked at the pants, then at the audience while at the same time ripping open the Velcro fastenings to remove the outer light-colored layer of pants from the front and back, revealing stylish black dress slacks.

Now Charlee had a whole new outfit. He looked like the pianist everyone had been expecting earlier. Charlee pointed at his shoes indicating that they were OK, pointed at the pants with the same OK gesture, looked at the jacket OK, took off the hat and looked closely at it before indicating that it was OK, as well. As Charlee removed the outfit, only two things remained the same. One was the white gloves that stayed on his hands at all times. The second was noticed when he snapped his finger and pointed to his face.

Charlee put his hands up to his face and started to pull on it as if he was pulling off the mask. Charlee pulled and tugged and tugged and pulled on his face as if wrestling with himself. As he pulled and tugged, he was pulling himself around the stage by his face. This pulling action took only a few seconds but at the end of this tug of war, Charlee could not remove anything from his face and gestured to the audience that the face had to stay as it was.

Charlee headed back to the piano, sat down on the bench and began to play. But what Charlee was playing did not make any sense at all. Everyone in the audience could tell that this music did not sound right. Charlee played for a few seconds until he realized something was wrong. Then, as he continued to play Charlee put his face closer to the music sheet for another look. He stopped playing and looked at the audience, putting one hand over his mouth he shrugged his shoulders as if saying, "Oops." He reached forward to get the music sheet and turned it right side up. This made everyone laugh, even Charlee.

Now the time had come for Charlee to get serious. His first selection of music was the school's fight song. The gym echoed loudly with the voices of the students as they sang along. By this time everyone backstage had stopped what they were doing to watch Charlee perform. Sam turned to Jeanie to whisper, "So far, so good. I was impressed with Charlee's performance as a comedian. Let's see if he's just as good at playing the piano."

The high school had set up a video camera to record the talent show. The principal, Mr. Harper, had planned to make copies of the film to send to the local TV stations. He hoped they would show some of the school program on the Philadelphia news. He thought that might encourage the other schools to start their own activity programs.

Charlee's second selection was a classic rock-and-roll favorite, *Blueberry Hill.* He followed it with *The Power of Love* and several more popular song before finishing with the musical piece known as *Unchained Melody.* Between each song the audience had been wild with their response. Charlee had to wait for several minutes for them to quiet and return to their seats.

Sam and Jeanie were thrilled with the reception Charlee was receiving. Every once in a while Sam would hug Jeanie. He didn't mention that he felt great relief mingled with his satisfaction. He thought to himself, "I'm sure glad Nick talked me into this." Then he suddenly realized that he had not seen Nick this evening.

Jeanie had been carefully watching Charlee perform. She was impressed by the way he was hitting the piano keys with such precision, making each note sound so loud and clear while he was wearing gloves. She thought it was amazing that he could be funny at one point and then change to serious concentration to play with passion and grace.

Sitting on the bleachers, Mr. Harper and the school board were amazed that such a professional performer was a part of a high school talent show. The Chairman of the School Board, Mr. Styffer, asked if Charlee was getting paid for his participation. Mr. Harper replied that no one on the program received a fee. Mr. Styffer wondered why anyone with such talent would perform for free. He even wondered how Charlee had been persuaded to come to a high school talent show. These comments puzzled Mr. Harper, who promised to find the answers before the end of the evening

Charlee was finished with the easy-listening portion of the performance. Everything was going exceptionally well. He was now slightly over the time allowed for each performer but no one seemed to notice. He wasn't finished, now it was time for dessert.

Charlee started putting his magical fingers to a real workout. The first selection of classical music was *Piano Concerto No. 1 in B Flat Minor* by Tchaikovsky. Before the show, Charlee had requested that when the classical portion of the program began that the lights on the audience be dimmed and a spotlight shined in the direction of the grand piano. As Charlee played these classical selections his scarred fingers hit every key with clear precision. Those magical fingers were dancing on the ivory keys with such speed it was truly unbelievable.

The audience realized that Charlee was not just another pianist, but a truly great artist. The School Board was so impressed that they had stopped making notes about the evening's progress. It was hard for them to believe that they were at a high school program. They felt as if they were at a concert and were being entertained by a famous pianist. They actually felt underdressed for the occasion.

Between musical selections the chairman, Mr. Styffer, asked the principal, Mr. Harper, how they had managed to obtain Charlee's service. He indicated that he would like to meet Charlee after the end of the show. Mr. Harper had to reply that he would ask Sam to arrange an introduction.

Charlee's last musical piece for the evening was *Moonlight Sonata No. 14 in C Sharp Minor* by Beethoven. He was playing with such masterful talent that the audience watched every movement in a mesmerized state. Charlee had gone past his allocated time by 45 minutes. The program had been scheduled to end around 10:00 and some of the concerned parents had begun calling the school to ask why their children hadn't returned home. No one in the gym had noticed the extra time. They could hardly wait to tell their parents about the program they had enjoyed.

When his performance finally came to an end, Charlee gave a bow to the audience. The gym exploded with applause and whistles and everyone stood in a wild ovation. Even the people behind the stage gave their share of applause. There was no doubt that Charlee's promise of an excellent performance had been fulfilled. When he stepped behind the curtains, leaving the stage, the audience was still applauding and cheering. Charlee had no choice but to go back on stage and give another bow. This was to be the beginning of a tradition for the remainder of Charlee's career.

While Charlee was giving his final bow his eyes misted and he whispered, "This applause is for you, Sister Clara. Thank you for the use of your magical fingers."

5

Sam would be happy to take full credit for Charlee's presence in the program tonight. But at this moment he was standing with all the other people who were anxious to meet the pianist. Backstage, the applause started up again, this time it was coming from the people working in the show to indicate their appreciation to Charlee. Charlee in return gave them a bow. How excited everyone was about the way the evening had turned out. They were all trying to talk to Charlee at the same time.

Sam suddenly remembered that Nick had told him Charlee was mute. "Attention, people," shouted Sam. "Please let's have some silence." Sam was trying to quiet everyone down. "May I have your attention. Please folks, please quiet down." It took a couple of minutes to get everyone to co-operate. "I'm sorry to say," Sam continued to speak to the people backstage, "Charlee is unable to speak. Charlee is mute."

That started everyone talking at the same time again, expressing their frustration because they were denied the opportunity to communicate with Charlee. "We will have to find a way to talk with Charlee," said Sam. "But before Charlee leaves, I want to thank him personally for participating in our talent show." Sam didn't notice that he was still referring to Charlee as male.

As Sam shook Charlee's hand he said, "Thank you for coming tonight, Charlee. You certainly had me worried for a while. I was afraid you weren't going to come. That was an excellent performance you gave us," before Sam could say more the people backstage started applauding Charlee again and when they finished Sam resumed his private conversation. "I am glad you decided not to use the music I gave to Nick. Your selections were perfect. I liked the way you divided the music for the different generations of the audience. Nick was right about your talent. He said you were a better pianist than the one I had scheduled before. I'm delighted it turned out the way it has." Sam's gratitude was visible in the smile that spread across his face.

The area backstage was becoming crowded as people from the audience rushed to get a closer look at this entertainer. The students were fascinated with Charlee's outfit, they wanted to examine the parts that had made him appear like a hobo, but they were disappointed because now he appeared in the dress version of the jacket and pants.

Charlee had a pen and notepad in his pocket to use for communicating. He didn't know if anyone would be available to translate who knew sign language. So Charlee wrote out his first question, he asked if anyone in the crowd knew sign language. He handed the note to Sam to be read to the crowd. It was fortunate that one person in the crowd, a teacher named Nancy, understood sign language.

As she moved closer, Charlee asked in sign language if she would translate. She was more than happy to help. She was excited that she was the one honored to help him. Charlee explained to Nancy that he was able to hear the questions so she was only needed to translate the answers to the crowd. This was to save a lot of time.

As Nancy translated, Charlee began, "Thank you for having me here and letting me entertain you. You were a great audience. You showed a great appreciation for my performance and I am grateful." Looking at Sam he continued, "I'm sorry if I had you worried earlier this evening, but I felt it would take too much time to write all the answers to your questions if I had revealed myself. Besides, it would have taken all of the fun out of the surprise I had planned for you."

"Nick asked me to let you know that he is sorry that he was unable to be here. He was not feeling well enough to come this evening. I have only a few minutes to spare before I must leave, I have another engagement to go to."

This wasn't true, but Nick was a little uneasy with his first appearance in disguise. He didn't want to take any more chances than he had to fearing that Sam might see through the disguise. "Does anyone have a question for me?" he asked as Nancy translated.

"Charlee," a loud voice echoed from the heavy crowd, "My name is Mr. Harper. I'm the principal of this high school. May I say that I thought you were just magnificent? I can't thank you enough for coming to our school to perform. We have never had a performer with such great musical talent in our school. I would like to introduce the school board members if I may. They are especially grateful to you for your performance in one of their public schools." Mr. Harper proceeded with the introduction of the school board members to Charlee. Some of the members seemed awed when introduced to such a fabulous character as Charlee.

The video camera was recording as the questions were being asked, especially by the students who were quicker to speak, the adults barely had a chance to get a word in. A student who wrote for the school's newsletter even had the bravery to ask a question no one else had the nerve to voice. "You cover your identity very well Charlee, I noticed that you are very graceful in all of your movements. It's really hard to tell whether you are male or female because of your outfit and the fact that we don't have your voice to give us any clues. The name Charlee as spelled in the program could indicate that a person of **either** sex would be able to use the name. So my first question is, are you male or female? The second question I would like to ask is, what is your reason for having the two different outfits, one as a hobo and the other as a traditional pianist."

The crowd waited with curiosity for Charlee's answers to the questions the student had asked. Several people in the crowd were mumbling under their breath about the rude questions. Charlee responded, "Someone here is probably thinking that you are either brave or crazy for those questions. But I find you to be honest and aware of things that others cannot see or understand. I predict that you will become an excellent reporter. So I will answer part of your questions, but not in the way you would have wanted me to answer."

The crowd was restlessly waiting for answers from Charlee. "The answer to both questions is that I would like keep my identity anonymous. I will leave the question of whether I am a male or a female to the imagination of my audience. Yes, Charlee is spelled so that **either** sex would be able to use the name. I would prefer, for personal reasons, not to discuss my costume at this time."

Everyone in the crowd was talking, repeating the questions and the answers to each other. Nancy was on cloud nine, she could not believe that she was translating for Charlee. This would be a memory that she would treasure forever, especially when he turned and told her what a fantastic job she was doing.

The man who had been standing beside the principal stepped forward to introduce himself, "My name is Mr. Styffer, I am the chairman of the school board. We were here tonight to do research to determine if the benefits of an after school program were worth the expense to the school budget. After seeing and hearing all of the performances this evening we, the school board, agree that the expense is justified. I would also like to ask if you would consider performing at our other schools. A pianist of your talent probably has many requests for his time, but we would like for you to consider the proposal.

Charlee's response was, "I would be happy to perform again at other schools, but my schedule will only permit me to volunteer for a limited time. I hope that other talented performers will also consider giving some of their own time for a worthy cause. Hopefully I am only the first of many." Charlee wrote down the number of a post office box where he could be contacted. "I need at least three weeks notice prior to the date you would like for me to perform," Charlee said in sign language as he handed the note to Mr. Styffer. After thanking Nancy for her help he signed, "I have to leave for my next engagement."

As Charlee neared the exit a young lady in a wheelchair blocked his path. As he looked at her she held out a pen and pad asking him for an autograph. Charlee was stunned; this was the first time he had ever been in a situation like this. Charlee smiled and took the pad from the young lady. He quickly wrote a poem and signed it. When she read the poem she smiled at Charlee who then gave her a wink and quickly ducked out the exit.

• • •

Monday at work when Nick walked into the music store Sam was talking about the performance that Charlee had given on Friday night. Sam saw him and quickly went over to say, "Thank you, Nick. You and Charlee have made me a happy man. Charlee was simply fantastic Friday night. I couldn't stop thinking about his performance all weekend. Why didn't you come Friday night?" Sam asked as if he didn't already know the answer.

"Oh" Nick said, "I wasn't feeling well, that's why I missed work Friday."

"Well you don't know what you missed," said Sam while laughing. Sam wanted to repeat his story to everyone in the store. When he spotted Mr. Gosby, the assistant store manager, he called out to him, "I want to tell you about Friday's show." So Nick was able to escape with a smile, pleased that Sam was satisfied with his performance.

That same Monday, Mr. Harper sent copies of the videotape to the city's TV stations. Some of the stations were not interested, but there were a couple of stations that agreed to include a mention of the talent show in the local news. At one station the evening news anchorwoman was a reporter named Paula. She had seen the film and was as fascinated with Charlee as everyone else had been when they saw him perform. She was intrigued on both a personal and professional level. She wanted to meet him, hoping for an interview.

Paula wanted the public to see what she had noticed in Charlee's performance. She believed that she was witnessing the start of a great entertainment career. Because her feelings had proved to be generally accurate in the past, she had learned to follow her hunches. Paula knew she needed more facts about the talent show. She wanted to interview the people who had been responsible for organizing the show to present the topic as a program sponsored by the school.

When Paula interviewed Mr. Styffer, chairman of the school board, he was happy to inform her that Charlee would be performing the next month at another high school. Her excitement was mixed with disappointment when she discovered that no one knew how to contact Charlee except by the use of a post office box address.

It appeared that Paula would have to wait a month for an interview with this extraordinary character. Paula also interviewed the high school principal, Mr. Harper, as she attempted to gather background information about Charlee. He was the person to name Sam as a contact close to Charlee. It seemed to Paula that she was going in circles when Sam told her it was Nick who was responsible for getting Charlee to come to the school to perform. So Paula tried to get an interview with Nick, who avoided Paula like the plague.

She finally gave up trying to schedule an interview with Nick because of the limited time before her broadcast scheduled for the next evening. Paula had put together a news segment about the school's talent show, beginning with the reasons for the evening program at the school. She showed a short portion of the video featuring the students' performance. She allowed a longer time period to show video clippings of Charlee performing in both his comedy and musical sections. Paula thought the interview with the student reporter important because of Charlee's response to the questions. She apologized to her viewers because she had not been able to get an interview with Charlee, stating that she planned to interview him the next month following his second performance.

Before Paula had finished her evening newscast, the phones at the TV station were ringing with calls from viewers wanting to know where Charlee would be performing next. Only a special story told by a good reporter like Paula could get a response as quickly as the calls were coming. As an ironic illustration of exactly how good Paula was, she knew even before Nick did, where Charlee would be performing next month.

During her interview with Mr. Styffer she had learned about an invitation that had been made to Charlee by the school board. Paula did her homework extremely well because the day the broadcast was shown was the same day that Nick received the letter requesting his second performance. The invitation was for a show scheduled the next month, the letter gave only the date and location of the program, but it concluded that more details would follow.

"Good," thought Nick, "The more performances I do, the more recognition Charlee will get." Nick was happy that he had begun his career plans by performing for the schools. He needed the month before his next performance to work on some new ideas for the show. He didn't want to do the same performance twice in a row. He knew that a few changes would make his part of the show more interesting.

Part of the changes that Nick planned for his second performance was the addition of recorded orchestral music as background to some of the classical selections of piano music. Nick believed that this would greatly enhance the sound of music coming from the piano. As Nick was experimenting with different types of make-up he thought of his ex-cellmate and friend, Mark. All of Nick's knowledge about disguise and make-up had been learned because of the generosity of his friend. He hasn't forgotten his teacher, whenever he had time available he would return to the prison to see Mark. Nick always took plenty of goodies and books when he went to visit. This was his way of extending his friendship and thanking Mark for the make-up skill he had learned. Nick had not confided his creation of Charlee even though Mark had made him possible.

As Nick was working on his disguise another person came into his mind. "I wonder what Teresa is doing right now?" he thought. He set aside his makeup to spend a moment daydreaming about her, "Behind the appearance of a sophisticated librarian was a good-looking young lady, with a sweet personality. Any man would find her very attractive," Nick said to himself. He spent a lot of effort trying not to think about her, but found that it was an impossible attempt to avoid situations where nature over-ruled his head.

Recently, Teresa had been popping into Nick's head more frequently than she had in the past. "What's happening to me?" Nick questioned himself with concern. "I don't have the time to get involved right now," he must remind himself of his plans. Nick didn't want to admit that what he felt toward Teresa had gone past simple liking. Nick had never before been in a situation like this and he didn't know that he couldn't control the feelings that overwhelmed him when Teresa came to mind.

The following day the second letter arrived from the school board, giving the rest of the information that Charlee needed for the performance. With the information package, came three special seating tickets. Mr. Styffer had realized that because there was no charge for the program the school would be overwhelmed with curious, music-hungry people wanting to see Charlee perform. He expected so many people that everyone would be packed into the gym like sardines in a can.

Due to the publicity from the TV station and the comments from the audience who had already seen Charlee perform, interest had spread like wildfire in the city of Philadelphia. Mr. Styffer, chairman of the school board, had a meeting with the principal of the high school, Mr. Chan, where Charlee would be performing to offer a few suggestions about crowd control. He recommended that tickets should be given in advance for admission to the program. They had determined how many tickets could be given to guests and representatives of the press in addition to those given to the students and faculty of the school. Mr. Styffer had been a witness to Charlee's last performance and recommended getting some security officers to admit only persons holding a ticket. "I'm sure that following Charlee's next performance many people from the audience will attempt to go backstage," stated Mr. Styffer, "So we must be able to control the situation or Charlee may not want to perform at our schools again."

Mr. Chan was in charge of arranging reserved seating for the special guests that had been invited.

This section would include the mayor's family and other important people invited by the school board members themselves. Mr. Styffer also suggested that it would be appropriate to send several tickets for the reserved area to Charlee.

When Nick received the tickets he knew immediately what he wanted to do. Two days later, Teresa received an anonymous letter with an invitation, three tickets and all the information she needed about the program. There was no indication where the tickets had come from or who had sent them, not even a return address. After the first wave of curiosity regarding her benefactor had past, Teresa realized that she had received tickets to the reserved area. Following that realization was the thought that someone considered her to be special enough to send her these tickets.

She had heard about Charlee from gossip at the library where she works. She was excited about going to see the entertainer everyone had been talking about. Teresa was excited because now she would have an excuse to ask Nick to accompany her to an evening program. She didn't want him to view her invitation as a date, so she was relieved that she had three tickets and could also invite a girlfriend from work to go along. "I'm sure Nick has heard of Charlee because he plays the piano," thought Teresa.

At her next piano lesson, she asked Nick if he would go to the program with her. She explained that she had received three tickets in the mail and didn't know who had sent them. Then she asked Nick if he had heard about Charlee. She mentioned that everyone was talking about his first performance. The people who had not seen it in person had seen the TV news report about it.

Nick, pretended ignorance, repeated Charlee's name several times in a low voice, shook his head at the same time as if he were trying to recognize the name and person. Then he said, "No, I've never heard of Charlee."

Teresa took this as encouragement to tell Nick what she had heard about Charlee. "I've heard that Charlee was simply fantastic. I also heard that he wants to remain anonymous behind the outfit. I think that's exciting," said Teresa. "I've always loved the roles of those characters on TV that had two separate identities with two faces, like Zorro and the Scarlet Pimpernel. They have always fascinated me," stated Teresa then added, "The mystery adds to the overall excitement." So Teresa repeated the question to Nick again. "Would you escort us to see Charlee perform." Teresa was thinking that Nick would want to go to the program because there was a piano involved.

Teresa caught Nick off-guard with her invitation. In the second before he replied he had to quickly think of an answer, so he stalled her by asking, "When did you say this show was supposed to take place?" When Teresa gave Nick the date and place Nick responded, "Oh, Teresa, I'm sorry but I've promised to be somewhere on that Friday evening. You'll just have to find someone else to go with you. But thank-you for the invitation, just the same." Nick was able to say this with a sad voice. He did feel guilty when he saw Teresa's excitement diminish.

Then she said, "Oh well, I just thought…" never finishing her statement. Rejection to Teresa was as painful as pouring alcohol on an open wound; she could not take rejection lightly. She turned the subject by suggesting that they needed to continue her lesson. Nick could see the disappointment written all over her face, but there was nothing he could do about it.

'Maybe the next time Teresa," said Nick, trying to cheer her up before they continued with the lesson.

6

Nick was ready for "Charlee" to perform at the next engagement. He had worked very hard to master the addition of the recorded orchestral music as background to his performance. On Friday, the day of the program, he planned to leave work early to take the needed equipment to the school. Nick had gone to a great deal of expense to get the right equipment for the sound effects necessary to harmonize both piano and background music. Included in the last letter from the school board was the information that there would be a grand piano available for Charlee's use. Finally the evening had arrived for the second performance of Charlee's new career. Not surprisingly, sitting on the bleachers in the gym, were some of the same people that had been at his first performance. Thirty minutes before the program was to begin the gym was already packed with an anxious crowd waiting to see Charlee. He had been the topic of many discussions. The special seating section was being filled with important guests; the mayor and his family had yet to arrive.

Paula was only one of the reporters from the several TV stations represented with film crews. They were all waiting for the time to start their cameras rolling, each one was hoping to get an interview with Charlee. Nick had written a letter to Mr. Chan, the principal of the high school where he was to perform. He began with a statement of apology because he was not able to communicate verbally due to his mute condition. Nick requested a room where Charlee would be isolated between his arrival and the time for him to perform. He explained his worry that his appearance would cause a distraction to the audience which would not be fair to the students scheduled before him, taking away some of their time of glory.

Nick knew that communicating in a letter would be difficult because it took more time to get his point across. He had given Principal Chan a precise time for his arrival so that Charlee could be met in front of the school. Then Charlee would be escorted to the waiting room. Principal Chan had agreed that this was a good idea and his office had been chosen as Charlee's refuge.

Teresa and two of her co-workers had found their way to the school gym. They presented their special seating tickets to one of the half-dozen security officers that the school had provided to help direct traffic and control the crowd. Each special ticket was numbered to match to a particular seat. Teresa's tickets were for the front row. This caused Teresa to wonder, "Who thinks I am important enough to be in this special seating area?" She became excited when the security officer escorting them to their seats said that she and her companions would be sitting with the mayor.

This sent goose bumps all through Teresa's body as she again wondered who was responsible for this. Teresa whispered to herself, "Thank you, whoever you are." While removing her coat, Teresa glanced at the people sitting on the bleachers and thought to herself. "Wow, there sure are a lot of people here tonight and there are more arriving every minute." After Teresa sat down, she looked up at the stage as the adrenaline started running excitedly all through her body. She knew she was one of the lucky ones that would actually be able to see Charlee up close. She was sad that Nick was not able to be here with her. She knew he would enjoy seeing Charlee perform.

Cheers from the audience broke Teresa's concentration. As she looked back to see what all the commotion was about, she could see that the mayor and his family were entering the gym while waving to the audience and the TV cameras. There were only two seats separating Teresa from the mayor's party. Paula and her cameraman followed the mayor. She began her interview with the mayor, first asking him about the after school program. Then before he could answer she quickly followed with another quick question. She asked if he had ever seen Charlee perform before.

The mayor looked at the camera and smiled before he turned to Paula. He responded by saying that he was honored that his family had been invited by Mr. Styffer and school board members. He spent several minutes giving his opinion about the after school program. He ended his remarks by saying, "No, I have never heard of Charlee prior to his last performance. Although I did get a glimpse of him on your evening newscast awhile back and what I did see of Charlee I found to be very exciting." Then he added, "When the school board invited me to attend this evening they explained the importance of these programs."

"They also included the information that there would be a professional pianist who disguises him or herself as a hobo. I was flattered by the invitation and delighted to be an honored guest. I am interested in seeing this talented performer. I understand that Charlee lives in our fair city. I know just from what I have seen and heard that Charlee will become very popular here in Philadelphia and hopefully throughout the USA in time."

After the interview with the mayor, Paula turned to Teresa because she wanted to get some feedback about Charlee from people in the audience. Paula wanted to hear her reason for coming to the school program. Teresa responded with the answer that she had received the tickets for this show from an anonymous donor. Then she stated that she had come especially to see Charlee because of all the exciting things she had heard about him. "The most amazing part," Teresa exclaimed, "Is that Charlee has only performed one show before. To see someone become so popular in one month's time would cause anyone to want to come and see Charlee perform for themselves, just to end their curiosity."

Outside in front of the school, Principal Chan was waiting for Charlee. When he arrived the principal introduced himself and gave Charlee an oriental bow, which was a tradition in Chan's native country, indicating a welcome to Charlee and his pleasure to make his acquaintance. Charlee responded with a bow, also showing his respect for Mr. Chan's tradition and then added a handshake.

Principal Chan remembered from his letter that Charlee was mute. He said to Charlee, "We are truly honored with your presence. You would not create any distractions by waiting in my office. I will see that you are not disturbed until I call on you a few minutes before you are scheduled to go on stage. If I'm a little late getting back to you, don't worry. NO one is going to leave without first seeing you perform," Chan stated with a little laughter.

"I have arranged for a person by the name of Linda to be here with me to translate for you. It appears that she is running late but I'm sure she'll find her way here shortly. In the meantime please just relax. There are refreshments in the refrigerator, if you care for some." Before Mr. Chan left the room, he turned and said, "I really do relish your outfit. Someone did a magnificent job putting it together." He then closed the door behind himself. Nick was left with a feeling of joyful anticipation.

Paula had been roaming around backstage hoping to get an interview with Charlee before he went on the stage. But he could not be found. Paula asked each person she met, but no one else had seen Charlee.

Linda, the woman Mr. Chan had asked to translate sign language for Charlee had arrived. Knocking on the door before she walked into the office, the first thing that burst out of Linda's mouth was, "What a magnificent outfit. You look stunning!" She said it with such exuberance, then immediately apologized for being late while introducing herself, practically all in the same breath. Charlee just smiled and in sign language said to Linda, "It's OK. I only need you to be with me when the show ends. Thank you for volunteering to help me."

Principal Chan entered his office to let Charlee know that there remained only two minutes before his appearance. He escorted Charlee to the gym and as they both entered the people who saw Charlee started cheering and applauding while whistles filled the air. It was fortunate that the performers scheduled before Charlee were finished because everything came to a halt due to the overwhelming noise. This magnificent hobo character was the reason that most of the people in the audience had come to see the program.

Those people who had not seen Charlee enter the gym were puzzled by all the ruckus, looking around curiously to see what was happening. No one in the special seating section had been able to see Charlee enter and they were startled by the sudden outbreak of noise. When Teresa realized that Charlee had entered the gym, her heart started pounding faster with excitement. With the audience making such a ruckus Teresa's adrenaline was running out of control.

Paula, from experience, knew right away that Charlee had entered the gym. She grabbed her camera operator and rushed backstage hoping to get a few shots of the peoples' reaction the moment they saw Charlee for the first time. She also wanted to get a closer look at Charlee for her own satisfaction.

When Paula finally had her first look at Charlee she almost forgot why she was there. She just stood there staring at this super looking character disguised as a hobo. When she finally snapped out of her temporary paralysis she motioned to her cameraman to start filming Charlee; she forgot her intentions to catch the reactions of the people around her. She wanted to keep the camera on Charlee for as long as possible.

As Charlee was waiting for the stagehands, who had fallen behind schedule, to complete the setup on stage he turned toward the rolling camera. Paula was amazed at what she saw, Charlee smiled and gave her a wink causing her knees to weaken. In all her years as a professional reporter she could not recall ever getting this excited over any other story in the past. Just then a security officer approached Paula and asked her if she would please wait until after the program ended get her interview.

Nick had gone to the school earlier that day to visit with Principal Chan, he explained that he had been requested to bring musical equipment for Charlee to use at tonight's show. Because he had other commitments he would not be able to come back in the evening to arrange the equipment. Nick had asked Principal Chan to pick a couple of trustworthy students, so that he could explain to them in advance how to put everything together and how to set it up that evening. He even anticipated that they might forget how to put some of the parts together and he had drawn a diagram for them to clarify the setup. He made arrangements with Principal Chan to pick up the equipment Saturday. Then Nick thanked him for his assistance and left.

As anticipated the students had encountered a little difficulty with some of the equipment and that had caused them to fall behind schedule. As they finished the announcer started to introduce Charlee. The lights dimmed as the words everyone had been waiting to hear were shouted over the intercom. "And now ladies and gentlemen. I give you Charlee." The gym was roaring with applause and any other sound the audience could make to show their welcome.

Charlee walked out from behind the curtains with the audience still applauding, using his arms to indicate to the audience, "That's right, let me hear more of your cheers and applause. More, more, louder, louder…."

As Teresa saw Charlee come out from behind the curtains, she turned her head toward the friends who were sitting beside her. Her face wore a shocked look as she realized, "I know him. He was in my apartment building." Then catching herself babbling she turned back to apologize for her outburst, explaining in a quivering voice that she didn't really know Charlee like it sounded, but that she had only seen him in her apartment building one evening.

Teresa was trying to explain herself to those around her who were looking at her strangely. Her hands were trembling uncontrollably from the surprise and excitement of seeing this same hobo character that had stood next to her in the elevator of her apartment complex. Teresa shook her head in disbelief and smiled as she thought to herself, "All this time I've heard of Charlee and didn't realize he was the same hobo I had seen."

Charlee was doing his usual routine to make the audience laugh. Then he walked to the edge of the stage where Teresa was sitting and stared at her momentarily, gave her a "hello again" wink. Amazingly, Teresa responded without thinking with a wink of her own. She blushed and at the same time put one hand over her mouth. Finally she removed her hand to wave and show Charlee her special smile. Her body language seemed to be asking Charlee if he remembered her. Charlee smiled as if answering, yes. Teresa had gone into the melt-down stage and was ready to slide off her chair.

Charlee finished the comedy portion of the show with his amazing changeover. The audience was overwhelmed by the way he accomplished this and also by his new appearance. Now he was ready to put the icing on the cake. He started off as before with playing the school's fight song. Charlee played a variety of musical selections that fit the younger generation but even the adult audience were enjoying the music. He played so well that the audience was moving with the rhythm of the music and tapping their feet. When he added some exciting honky tonk music he had some of the audience itching to get up and dance.

Charlee's performance really had Teresa's attention, not only because he played so well, but also because the style and movements were so similar to Nick's style. Yet Teresa had never heard Nick play this type of music. "Oh, you're just being silly," she thought to herself.

After entertaining the younger generation, it was now time to entertain the more mature audience. This time Charlee planned to have recorded orchestral music in the background to enhance the sound of the piano. All this had to be done with precise timing. Nick had needed a lot of practice to perfect the timing for the addition of the orchestral music. He used the sound of clicks prior to the start of the music. Two clicks let him know he had five seconds before the music started to play, one click let him know there were two seconds left. Nick had to count to himself once the last click sounded to get the right timing to begin to play. Nick had an electronic hand-held control so that he could start and stop the tape.

Timing was very important to this type of musical performance. If the timing was lost so was the performance. This would be a disaster to the program and an embarrassing moment for Charlee. This was one of the reasons Nick had thought about having a partner. It was both complicated and time-consuming to do everything by himself. Having a partner would surely make things a lot easier. But this evening he blocked these distracting thoughts from his mind so his performance could be perfect.

Charlee started with the musical selection *Moonlight Sonata No. 14 in C Sharp Minor No. 2* by Beethoven. The sound of the clicks alerted him as he sat on the bench waiting for the right moment to start playing. When the music started Charlee was ready to give the audience a performance they would never forget. The gym echoed with the sound of music coming from the large speakers that Nick had purchased for this and other performances. Then the sound of the piano started interweaving with the music.

Nick was right about the orchestral music enhancing the music from the piano with a much greater meaning for the audience. Anyone who walked into the gym and heard the music that was being played would have thought that they had walked into a concert hall. As Principal Chan was waiting for Charlee's next selection a thought came to his mind, "People would pay a lot of money to listen to a performance like this. We are fortunate to have such a performer in our school at no cost." Then he erased all thoughts and returned to listen when the music resumed.

Charlee's fingers moved so elegantly on the piano keys that they made his performance look easy. His love of playing the piano was the strong point he had used to learn how to have full control of his distorted fingers. His fingers hit every key with so much meaning and with such skillfully precise timing that everyone was awed that he could do this while his fingers were laced in white silk, tailored-made gloves. Magical fingers in white would be the best way to describe Charlee's artistic fingers.

It was almost as fascinating to watch Charlee play as it was to listen to him play. The way his arms would sway with his body as if he were conducting a symphony had everyone fascinated. The glow of undeniable satisfaction was visible beneath his makeup while those magical fingers danced and picked out perfect tones on the ivory keys. No one would have ever thought that the character who dressed up like a hobo and performed a comic routine would also play music as remarkable as their ears were hearing. That was what made this whole concept so overwhelming, it left everyone to wonder who was this talented person behind the two conflicting outfits. They were also wondering if this person was male or female.

When Charlee finished playing the second piece of classical music you would have thought it was his finale the way the audience cheered and applauded, giving him a standing ovation that should have been saved for last. Principal Chan and the mayor had the same reaction to the music as the rest of the audience. This was the first time they had ever heard Charlee play and his talent amazed them. The mayor was so impressed he was almost speechless. If he had been asked for a comment by the media at this very moment, he would have been at a loss for words.

It took a few minutes for the audience to settle down as Charlee waited patiently to continue. He loved the reaction of the audience.

While Charlee had been playing his first classical selection piece, Teresa sat there in awe. She was moved by the sound of the orchestral music in harmony with the piano. Her eyes and ears were telling her that the style of the performer she was watching was identical to Nick's style. "After all, I should know, I have heard Nick play so many times. I know the movements he makes with his arms and hands and the sway of his body from watching him demonstrate some of my lessons."

Hearing Charlee play reminded her of the times she would stand by Nick's apartment door listening to him play. Hearing him play would take her breath away and put her into a musical dreamland. This was when she truly felt love for the first time in her life. She had secretly fallen in love with the masterful pianist who had literally swept her off her feet with the beautiful music that he played. Nick would start to play his piano from the minute he walked into his apartment until around ten o'clock. He would play for long hours at a time on his days off from work. She had heard him so many times that she even heard him playing in her sleep.

Teresa started to think the unthinkable. Questions were filling her mind. "If I had not seen Charlee in the elevator that one evening, I wouldn't be as suspicious as I am now that Nick and Charlee are the same person. It's really an easy puzzle if you have all the pieces and if you look closely at the whole picture. I wish there was a way to confirm my suspicions, but I don't want to intrude into Nick's privacy."

"I wish I could be a part of this to help him. I would do anything just to be with the man that I love. I'm starting to understand why he has neglected me and why he turned down the invitation to come with me this evening. If my assumption was right Nick already had a secret date with his fans. Now I don't need to wonder any longer who sent me these tickets. I bet that Nick's handwriting would match the writing on the envelope that brought the invitation. Nick's identity will remain his secret, but I find this to be extremely exciting." Teresa's deep blue eyes were covered with tears of joy because she had ingeniously unraveled Nick's secret.

7

Paula had her cameraman film the entire program. The musical selection that Charlee played had left her breathless. She felt lucky to be present to witness his performance. She was still hoping that before she broadcast her story she would be able to interview Nick. She felt cheated because she had not been able to find him during the month that she had been pursuing him for a meeting. She thought that Nick might be the person who would act as the missing link, someone who knew everything about Charlee.

Her instincts had told her that Nick was hiding something because of the way he had been avoiding her. She believed that Nick knew Charlee's true identity. She would like nothing more than to reveal the person behind the disguise.

In the special seating area the mayor turned around to whisper to Mr. Styffer who was sitting behind him. "How did you ever get Charlee to perform in your schools? It would certainly be great to have him perform for the city's council Christmas party."

Mr. Styffer responded with a whisper of his own, "Yes that would be a great Christmas bonus to have Charlee perform at our party." The mayor smiled then turned back to face the stage. Charlee's performance was coming close to the end. The next musical piece would be *Piano Concerto No. 1 in F Flat Minor* by Tchaicovsky. Midway into this musical piece the audience appeared almost in a trance. Charlee was truly amazing, this musical selection was a perfect choice for this audience. He ended his performance with *Exodus*, a popular musical piece.

Charlee had given a moving performance of the best quality that evening. He received a standing ovation from the audience that lasted almost two and a half minutes. Again Charlee's tradition was to come out from behind the curtains for a second bow while the audience got louder. The cheers and whistles could be heard blocks away from the school gym. The noise was loud enough to cause residents around the school area to wonder what was happening in the gym to cause everyone to go wild. The mayor smiled as he looked around at the audience. He was amazed at how much everyone had enjoyed Charlee's performance.

With a runny nose and teary-eyes Teresa also stood up to give her applause and show her response to a delightful performance that had been given by Nick. "Oh, did I say Nick," she was thinking, "I'm sorry, I meant Charlee." The response from the audience was so loud in the gym that a few people thought the roof would come crashing down.

Charlee had to come out from behind the curtains to bow for the third time. His performance had been a delightful experience. Paula and her cameraman were catching the whole thing. She was narrating so that she could tell her viewers what an exciting performance it had been and show the loud response of the audience. She had to scream into her microphone to be heard over all the noise.

Paula wanted to be the first reporter to get to the mayor for a post-concert interview. She quickly asked what his thoughts were of the performance put on by Charlee. The mayor turned to Mr. Styffer and in a show of camaraderie, pulled him over to rest his arm around Mr. Styffer's shoulder. The mayor began his statement, "I again want to thank Mr. Styffer and the school board for requesting my presence at this sensational program. Every performer this evening did a tremendous job. I had to miss a very important meeting this evening to come down to this school's program. Trust me when I say it was worth my time."

"Charlee's performance was truly out of this world; it was simply breathtaking," the mayor expressed these sentiments with excitement in his voice. "I would love to see Charlee perform again. It's a real pity that he has yet to give our city enough concerts so that everyone who resides in Philadelphia could get to enjoy one of the city's finest entertainer and pianist. The City of Philadelphia really should not let talent like Charlee's get away.

Paula proceeded to ask the mayor for his thoughts about Charlee's wardrobe and how it was used to disguise him or herself. She asked if the mayor was curious to know who was behind the masterful disguise. The mayor answered, "It would be interesting, I repeat, only interesting to know who is behind the mask. But I feel that if the person behind the mask does not want to be known, then we should give this person the right to privacy. If we attempt to reveal the real identity of this performer we risk loosing his or her willingness to perform in the public eye. The public may lose their chance to enjoy this great entertainer who is also a masterful pianist. So the way I see it, it would be wise to leave a good thing alone."

When the mayor finished his carefully phrased comment, Paula cleared her throat sensing that there was a subtle warning to discontinue her efforts to penetrate Charlee's disguise. She quickly pulled the microphone away from the mayor and politely thanked him for his interviews and turned to go backstage hoping to get a long awaited interview with Charlee.

By now many of the people from the audience were also trying to get backstage for a closer look at this incredible performer. The aisles leading in that direction were filled with people nudging their way to get a closer look at Charlee. The security officers had their hands full trying to keep the people from overcrowding the area backstage, but found it to be impossible, there were too many people shoving their way through, trying to see this exciting pianist and entertainer who had musically played his way into their hearts.

Principal Chan had to go up on stage to use the microphone to ask, "Please, would everyone settle down and not try to come backstage. Now folks," Principal Chan pleaded, "Is this the way we treat our guest? Everyone please clear the area." Charlee stood waiting on the stage, he felt exuberant that the audience wanted to get a closer look at him.

In the meantime the mayor and Paula had made it up to the stage. Linda, who was to translate for Charlee, also arrived in one piece. The mayor quickly went over to introduce himself and shake hands with Charlee. He was careful not to squeeze too firmly on those magical fingers. As he spent a few minutes talking to Charlee, Principal Chan had made progress sending people away from the area. Charlee's fans had bumped into each other as they left, glancing back at Charlee as long as it was possible to see him.

After the mayor finally finished talking it was Paula's chance to interview Charlee. She had been anxiously waiting a month for this opportunity and she was suddenly speechless for a few seconds. She actually forgot what she wanted to say. She wasn't certain if the comments the mayor had made about respecting Charlee's disguise had changed her questions, or if the excitement of finally being face to face with this extremely talented character caused her a ten-second lapse of her memory. But because she was an excellent reporter, Paula reached deep within herself and found what was needed to regain her composure and introduce herself to Charlee. She began her interview; "The people of Philadelphia have waited in expectation for a month for your second performance. With your first appearance you performed with only a piano at the other high school and you were wonderful.

Now with your second performance you have added an orchestral background to some of your selections. I find that either way you perform your talent is simply overwhelming. But I can also see that the orchestral background enhances the music from your piano. It sounded as if the Royal Philharmonic Orchestra was here accompanying you. This evening's performance went beyond anyone's expectations. My question is, where did you learn to play the way you do?"

Charlee glanced toward Linda to make sure that she was ready to translate. Then he began, "Before I answer your question, Paula, I would like to thank the audience for showing how much they appreciate my performance. I would also like to thank the school board for the opportunity to perform for the schools.

I have special thanks to give to an angel who was named Sister Clara. She saw something in me that no one else ever saw and she believed in me. I am here only today because of this special angel's love. She was my first and my best teacher. And every time I sit down to perform, I feel the presence of her hands guiding my hands. She truly is my guardian angel." At that moment Paula noticed a glaze of tears in Charlee's eyes.

Nick never once mentioned that this had taken place in an orphanage. He feared that because Paula was a good reporter she would search for clues until she found Charlee's true identity. Paula continued to interview Charlee while Teresa remained sitting in her seat. She was watching Charlee throw answers and comments to Linda in sign language and was able to catch everything he was saying. She had been very interested in his comments about having a nun for his teacher. She thought this was like a fairy tale that one would read about.

Paula was happy with the interview with Charlee. She never did ask him about his disguise. She must have taken the advice of the mayor with these words repeating in her mind, "It's best to leave well enough alone."

The following day Nick was leaving his apartment headed for the elevator, he was going to his usual café to eat. As he neared he saw that Teresa was standing inside the elevator carrying a laundry basket full of clean clothes. Nick began to say hello and chat with her for a minute as they changed floors. Teresa quickly started the conversation, "Hi Nick, you don't know what you missed last night at the high school's talent show." And she started to tell him about the program.

Nick politely interrupted her by saying, "I was just going over to the café to have lunch. If you are interested in coming with me I'll buy you some lunch and you can tell me everything about last night's program."

"OK," she was quick to reply, "give me a minute and I will be with you." So Nick, being the gentleman, carried her basket of neatly folded clothes to her door. After she unlocked the door and sat the basket inside they both continued to the café for lunch. While they were eating, Teresa told Nick how fantastic the performance had been that Charlee gave at the school. "Charlee's performance was simply flawless. You had to have been there to understand how wonderful it was, Nick."

While Teresa was sharing her impressions of the performance with Nick, she tried to find a reaction when she talked about Charlee that might betray his identity. But she failed to notice anything unusual in Nick's behavior. When she finished giving all the details about the program she asked Nick, "Have you ever considered becoming a pianist professionally?"

Nick took a sip of his rich dark coffee then looked into Teresa's beautiful blue eyes and slowly answered, "Sure, but I feel I'm just not good enough to perform professionally at this time."

Nick and Teresa sat at the café for most of that afternoon talking about anything and everyone they could think of. Each had their own secret reason for wanting to be together. Everyone had a time when they just want to talk. This was their time. They had always felt comfortable just being with each other.

• • •

The following Monday at the music store, Nick was working on the sale of a grand piano to the mayor's wife. She was telling him that she and her husband had been planning to purchase a baby grand piano for a long time. "We both play the piano," she said proudly. "The mayor is always having some event at the house and we frequently end up gathered around the old upright piano.

After we heard Charlee perform Friday evening we were so excited about the majestic sounds that came from the grand piano he was playing that we both gave up on the idea of purchasing a baby grand piano and decided to get the grand piano instead. We read in the program that the piano had been donated for the school's use by this music store. We agreed that if this music store was generous in its donation of the use of one of their expensive pianos to benefit the city school system that generosity should be rewarded. We feel that one good deed deserves another, that's the reason for shopping at this store.

The mayor was hoping to have Charlee come to the house someday," she added to Nick in a whisper. "He would like to show off one of Philadelphia's finest entertainers, especially when special guests come to visit."

"I'm sure that Charlee would be more than happy to perform for the mayor," was Nick's hidden response of acceptance for Charlee to perform for the mayor.

• • •

That same Monday evening, Paula was anchoring the evening news. She made sure she would have enough airtime to show some clips from Friday's performance at the school that she had captured on tape. She had been given the approval by the station's management to hold her report past the weekend to gain a larger viewing audience. After she had completed the national and world news she began her special segment, "I have a special entertainer to share with all of our Philadelphia viewers." She started the videotaped interviews that had been done early Friday evening. She explained all the details and reasons for this program. After a few minutes narrating the students' part of the program she ended with praise for their efforts and talent.

Then Paula turned to the main subject that she had been eager to show. "I have a short film clip to show of one particular performer who gave of his or her time to perform at our schools. "Charlee" That's right. The name of this very talented performer is Charlee." Paula then started the clip of Charlee performing while he was wearing this unique hobo outfit. She showed the fascinating way he changed from his original disguise into a well-dressed pianist. She pointed out in her narration that the only things that did not change were the gloves and the mask of makeup.

She showed a few minutes of his performance of the popular music and then faded into the final selection of classical music performed with the orchestral background. When the eyes of her viewers were glued to the TV screen she ended the filmed segment by saying, "I'm sorry but we have run out of time to show more of the performance of this magnificent pianist." She continued, "On my Sunday morning program "What's Happening in Philadelphia" I will air a special segment on this performer. For those of you who have not heard or seen Charlee before this evening's newscast, you certainly don't want to miss my Sunday morning's program on this rising new star who resides here in our city of Philadelphia."

When Sunday morning arrived Paula opened her special, "Good morning and welcome to What's Happening in Philadelphia. My name is Paula and I will be your host this morning. We have a very special and interesting program today. I regret that we are unable to have "Charlee" here in person with us, however, we wanted to introduce this special artist to each of you.

I was amazed with professional ability displayed by this unique performer. One of the most interesting aspects of this story is that everyone I interviewed had never heard or seen Charlee before he performed a month ago. What I am about to show you was Charlee's first performance here at one of our Philadelphia high schools. We know very little about this remarkable performer. I can say that one of the fascinating parts of this character was that we don't even know if Charlee is male or female.

Everyone I have interviewed has generally talked about Charlee using the word "he" only because one usually views a hobo in a male sense. There is no disrespect intended here if this character is actually female. "Charlee" if by chance you are watching, I do apologize if any remark has appeared to be disrespectful.

I'm sorry to say that Charlee is mute. I do not know if Charlee has been mute since birth or if the condition was caused later from some past ailment. It makes no difference to me if Charlee is mute, or whether male or female.

What has impressed me was the unbelievable and remarkable talent that Charlee has. I would not have believed it myself if I had not been there to see and capture the event on film. I wanted to share this with you so that you may see for yourselves the impressive performance by this superb pianist. What added to this intriguing effect of the entertainer was the way he first appeared dressed as a hobo and changed his appearance right on stage in front of everyone. He became an elegant pianist, as you will see for yourself."

At that moment Paula began showing a clip of Charlee coming out from behind the stage curtains dressed as a hobo. appearing on TV for all to see. "Looking at this particular character dressed in his hobo outfit it was unremarkable when he performed in a comedic way. Without even saying a word he was able to make the audience laugh. But to me," Paula stated, "putting aside the comic act, I was looking at a character whom everyone visualized as being funny. The amazing thing was that when this same character appeared dressed in another outfit he sat in front of a grand piano and played on the level of a concert pianist and no one laughed. I want you to be as amazed as I was."

Paula continued to show more clips while narrating through the performance. Because it was an exciting and historic event for the fair city of Philadelphia the TV station management had decided to extend the normal time for one segment and give Paula extra time for completion of her clips and comments. After all, it wasn't every day that a rising new star like Charlee appeared in their city. This time the TV station was prepared for all the incoming phone calls that they expected to follow this special on Charlee.

8

On Sundays, the prisoners had a day off from their normal duties and were given extra recreation time from sun-up to sundown. Mark, Nick's friend and ex-cellmate, was lounging around the recreation room where the TV was located. It was a coincidence that the TV was tuned to the station where Paula's program was being shown. Mark was sitting at a distance from the TV when Paula started showing clips of Charlee performing.

When Mark caught a glimpse of Charlee dressed as a hobo he got up from where he sat lounging, stared at the TV screen momentarily and then started to walk hurriedly toward the screen. It seemed to Mark as if he were walking in slow motion and could not get to the TV fast enough. What seemed like long stretched minutes really only took seconds of time for him to travel from his chair to the TV and he sat down in amazement.

Mark was excited to look at the outfit that Charlee was wearing. After performing for 15 years as a clown in the circus the hobo disguise struck cords of familiarity. When the comedic routine was over he was in a relaxed and happy mood. Because he was comfortable on the couch he didn't quickly change the TV station when the classical music began. As he sat watching he began to realize that Charlee sounded like his friend, Nick, playing with the same style and rhythm.

Mark knew Nick's piano playing well; he remembered the times he would take a cigarette break while Nick would practice on the piano. While Nick played something that would be an ear-catching tune Mark would shake his head in disbelief that someone with so much talent be in a joint like this entertaining prisoners. "What a waste of talent," he thought.

As Mark continued to watch he noticed that when the camera zoomed in on Charlee's face the application of the makeup looked familiar. It's interesting how someone could recognize a familiar sight or sound, when Mark recognized the makeup technique it was the same as an artist recognizing his own work. The makeup on Charlee's face looked exactly like the way Mark applied his. It was also the way Mark had taught Nick to put on his makeup.

As Mark continued to watch he came to a conclusion, "There is only one person I know who plays like the character on TV. That person is Nick." Mark felt happy that his friend had gained recognition with his new career. This time he was entertaining the right crowd, not a group of prison inmates. Mark knew that with Nick's talent and ambition he would become a big success. Then Mark started to chuckle as he thought to himself, "I know a secret, but it is as safe as the gold in Fort Knox."

• • •

Teresa was also watching Paula's special. As she saw the program for the second time she was still excited that she had recognized that Charlee was really Nick wearing a disguise. She liked the idea that everyone else was still puzzled about the identity of Charlee. "I'm sure many out there wonder about the identity of this fantastic entertainer. Is this masterful pianist male or female, rich or poor, famous or just an ordinary person."

"This idea that they do not know who Charlee is and are left to guess makes this even more exciting. Maybe some day they would find out who the person behind the mask really is, but for now it's good to keep everyone in suspense. I'm sure it adds to his notoriety." Because Teresa was convinced that Nick and Charlee were the same person she was not surprised when she matched the handwriting on the envelope that had brought the tickets. With her suspicions confirmed she felt a little guilty for learning Nick's secret. She wanted nothing more than to spend her life with the person she loved. She was hoping to someday have the privilege of sharing all of his secrets.

Teresa suspected that Nick had unknown reasons that created the necessity to remain anonymous. She had become well aquatinted with Nick in these past years. After spending much time in thought she decided to confront him with her suspicions. "There is a way to approach any topic, I only need to find the right way to approach this one with Nick," she thought to herself.

She hoped Nick would calmly accept her knowledge of his secret identity because she suspected that he had begun to return her emotional attachment. Acting on the intuitive gift called through many generations, woman's intuition, she trusted her instincts about his feelings. Teresa wished that when the confrontation was over that Nick would take down his invisible shield and let her into his heart and into the arms that she had waited for so patiently.

She suspected that Nick had been holding back his affection for her because of the demands of his new career. She hoped that he would accept her as a partner in both his love and in his work. She wanted to add her strength to his to build his career.

Nick was having a similar discussion with himself. Following the last program he had decided that he needed a partner he could trust to help him with his performances. When he listed all of his requirements for a partner he wondered where he could find a person with those qualifications.

Teresa herself had been compiling a list. It was made of reasons she would give to Nick to prove their compatibility. In the time that she had known Nick they had never had a serious disagreement. She thought of the way he had started his career and approved of everything he had done; to her that proved that they had similar minds. Teresa knew she was very smart, she had proved it by opening the locked door to his secret world. She also had a good knowledge of music because she was still learning from the best teacher, Nick. Teresa had a generous heart and one big factor in her favor was that she knew sign language. These qualities to be a good partner were added to the fact that she was willing to help him in any way possible. The bonus she saved for last was that she truly loved him. What more would any one want in a partner?

That week as Nick picked up his mail at the post office, there was another invitation for Charlee to play for the school. Among his other letters was one that caught his attention. It was a letter from a company called Brenner and Brenner. Nick already knew what the school letter was about, so he saved it to read later at home. He was curious about the letter from Brenner and Brenner. Nick recognized the name as a company that dealt in real estate and owned many buildings in the city of Philadelphia. The music store that employed Nick was located in a building that was owned by this company.

Nick could not open the letter fast enough to ease his curiosity. The letter was written personally by Mr. Brenner, chairman of the board. The letter read, "Dear Charlee, I must apologize for the use of your post office box to offer you a business proposition. I was told that there was no other way to contact you. Mr. Styffer, a very close friend, gave me your address. Please do not hold Mr. Styffer responsible for this invasion of your privacy. I can be a very persuasive businessman and I take full responsibility for any inconvenience.

Last Sunday I saw "What's Happening in Philadelphia" with a feature about you. While watching your performance I realized that you would be perfect for the grand opening of my new mall. I persuaded Mr. Styffer to give me your post office box address so that I could invite you to perform for the public opening in two months time." In the envelope was a business card of Mr. Brenner with his private phone number that was only given to a few special people for important business deals. On the back of the card was written an additional special note. "Please, let's get together on this. You will be handsomely rewarded if you accept."

Nick was certainly excited about this special invitation. This would be his first paid professional job. Charlee's career appeared ready to take off. As he walked out of the post office building, he was stopped by a TV reporter. This reporter was from one of Paula's competing stations. He wanted a feature on Charlee following the success of her special. His intention was to ask for the public's view about the sensational Charlee who was gaining both recognition and popularity in the city of Philadelphia. The reporter asked Nick if he would answer a few simple questions and would he also give his comments about Charlee.

Nick was in a state of panic. "OH-NO," he thought. "They must have found out about me. But how?"

The reporter motioned for the camera to begin filming. He did his usual opening then turned to Nick to ask, "Sir, do you know about the entertainer named Charlee who has been performing at our city's high schools. He was seen on TV last weekend on a TV special. Have you ever seen him?"

Nick sighed with relief as his skin began to get back to its normal color. "Yes, sir," answered Nick. "I was fortunate to catch the special this past weekend on Charlee. I had heard about him before the special was aired but I had never had the opportunity to be at one if his performances. I was impressed by the media's quick response to this rising new star in our city of Philadelphia. It was amazing to see the character dressed as a hobo change to a totally different outfit, then perform on the piano with such magic. Charlee if you are watching, the public is waiting for a concert from you."

The reporter turned back to the camera to respond, "Thank you, sir for your comments." Then the camera was stopped as the reporter told Nick,. "That was very good. You were dong so well that I certainly didn't want to stop you. You can bet that your comments will be among those that are shown."

"I hope I didn't over do it," Nick thought as he laughed inside. "I hope none of the people I work with see this piece on TV. They would remember that I know Charlee personally. Oh well, if they mention anything about this interview, I will say that I was trying to give Charlee a bigger boost. No big deal". Nick shook his head then smiled while he headed home.

The station that had shown the special on Charlee was receiving a load of mail every day for him. His fans didn't know where else to mail their letters. It was difficult for the station to handle over-abundance of mail as it was gathered into sacks. They did not have enough room to store the sacks of letters and they didn't know what else to do except to describe the situation on the evening news.

In an effort to reach Charlee they made a plea for him to contact the station with his address. They planned to make an announcement so his fans could mail their letters directly to him. They also wanted to send the sacks of fan letters that had accumulated at the TV station. This small bulletin was shown briefly for several days during that week on the evening news with Paula. She had tried to get the post office box from Mr. Styffer, but he would not reveal the address.

Nick heard about this bulletin at the music store and he was excited about the fan mail response to his performances. After he calmed down he was suddenly confused about what he should do with all the fan mail. At this time he did not want the public to have Charlee's address. He knew that he wasn't organized to handle this problem. The fan letters would have to stay at the TV station temporarily.

Nick knew he would have to come up with something quick. He had never realized the difficulty involved with this secrecy. It was more complicated because he did not have anyone to help him with his affairs. That night while he laid in bed he thought of a solution to the problem with the fan mail. He would send a letter to Sam's daughter Jeannie. Charlee would ask Jeanie if she would start a fan club to take care of all the letters.

Nick knew he would have to go through a legal procedure with the post office for Charlee to give the fan club the right to accept Charlee's mail. Nick had confidence that Jeanie would be happy to help because this was what caused Jeanie to flourish.

"Now I hope that problem is solved. What I really need is to find myself a partner. History is filled with characters in disguise like Zorro, Batman and the Scarlet Pimpernel. They all had trusted partners to help in all their affairs. Having a partner would certainly take a lot of the weight off of my shoulders." The more Nick thought about his idea the more eager he became to find his partner.

"But who?" thought Nick. "Who do I know other than Mark. He is certainly unavailable at this time. Who else would I trust with my secret that could handle a variety of responsibilities." After he spent time racking his brain a strange thought took over his mind and a feeling of calm enveloped him. The thought was so clear that he wondered if it was visible above his head in flashing neon lights. He thought the lights should have flashed with enough brightness to catch the attention of a blind man. "Teresa." was the name in his mind.

Nick didn't even have to spend any time to consider this idea of Teresa as his partner. The very thought was soothing to his mind. He had been aquatinted with Teresa for several years. He believed that in those years he had gotten to know a lot about her. He knew that Teresa was someone he could trust. She was everything he wanted in a partner and he was confident she would be happy to help him. "I wish I knew why I didn't think of her before."

Nick was impatient to see Teresa. He was excited about the prospect that she might become his partner. An invitation for an early dinner on Saturday evening in his apartment seemed like a safe place to start. Teresa had always looked forward to any invitation from Nick for the opportunity to spend time with him.

She had also become aware of Nick's hidden ways of showing affection without even saying a word. Any invitation was an indication that he was thinking of her that she accepted as flattery.

When Saturday evening finally arrived Nick answered the knock on the door to find Teresa standing there dressed for a fine dinner in a classy restaurant. He was stunned by her radiant beauty. Hidden daily behind her drab librarian's uniform was a gorgeous woman.

He had spent the whole Saturday in preparation for this meal. He had wanted to make it a special occasion to present his propositions to Teresa. Cooking was Nick's second love, playing the piano being his first. If Nick had not become a professional musician he would have become a chef. This special dinner was a southwestern type of meal typical of the area where he had lived in the orphanage. The chicken enchilada casserole in a creamy sauce with green chiles was served with rice, beans, fried sopaipillas and finished with flan for dessert.

Teresa complimented the food as the two sat down to their evening meal. While eating they had their usual conversations about work, music and other topics. The soft sounds of their voices were spiced with laughter every once in awhile as the soft sound of music could be heard in the background. After finishing their meal, they both worked together to clear the table, wash the dishes and put everything away.

Not quite a glamorous end to the evening, but this had become a tradition they had developed over the years. Regardless of which apartment they ate at they both worked together in the style of a married couple to clean up.

9

Nick turned the radio off and turned to Teresa. "I have something very important to discuss with you and it will take some time. Let me make some coffee and we can sit in the living room while I tell you what's on my mind."

Teresa's mind was racing. Nick had never approached her in such a serious mood before. What was this important issue? She thought to herself, "Calm down and don't be so impatient."

After the two made themselves comfortable, Nick took hold of one of Teresa's hands and held it gently. "Teresa," he said in a low, soft voice. "You must promise that what I am about to reveal to you stays in this room when you leave and will never leave your lips."

Teresa's heart was pounding excitedly as Nick paused for an answer. Even though Nick knew she could be trusted without her answer he wanted her to say the words of trust as reaffirmation to herself. Teresa just sat there with a dazed and confused expression on her face. "Well, Teresa?" Nick asked again.

This gentle question snapped her out of her daze and she stuttered her answer. "Oh yes-yes I promise that what you tell me this evening will not leave this room or, for that matter, my lips."

Nick cleared his throat and began, "I have known you for about two years. In that time I feel I have learned a lot about you, more than you realize. There is not one day that has gone by that I haven't thought about you. You have always been so kind and good to me. You listen to me even when I am boring. I find you sweet, kind and honest and very trustworthy. You are truly a woman any man would want to have in his heart and in his life."

Teresa could not believe what her ears were hearing. She was flattered by the words she had never heard him say before. Nick continued, "I have always had a lot of trust in you and that's why I am coming to you with this delicate situation that I am about to reveal. Before I get to that I want to give you some history of myself and my past. You have always asked me to share information about my past years, but I wanted it to remain buried and dormant. Now I will tell you what I have been trying to conceal."

"I have had many good years but then there were also many dark and gloomy years I would rather have kept buried." Nick began telling Teresa about Sister Clara and the time spent in the orphanage. He told how Sister Clara had taken him under her wings and caring for him like a mother, teaching him piano lessons.

This reminded Teresa of the time Charlee had given an interview at the high school. Teresa remembered that as she was reading the sign language Charlee was relating to Linda that he had mentioned a special angel by the name of Sister Clara and gave her a special thank you. Teresa's heart was beating even faster with excitement as she realized that Nick was revealing himself.

As Nick continued his story how Sister Clara had been his guardian angel throughout his growing years at the orphanage. "There are times now when I can feel the presence of Sister Clara. She will always be in my heart." Nick paused briefly taking a few deep breaths in order to keep from breaking into tears. Realizing the hurt in Nick, Teresa gently squeezing his hand in a loving gesture to say it's OK to cry.

After regaining his composure Nick continued to tell Teresa everything about his life up to the time he finished college and said his good-byes to Sister Clara. "I had the attitude that I was going out to conquer the world," Nick expressed himself proudly.

Now came the dreadful time to tell Teresa about becoming an alcoholic and of his time living on the streets. So Nick took a deep breath and started his story again. "I was very comfortable performing with this small orchestra here in Philadelphia but in six months time I was terminated.

"In plain English, I got fired.

"The reason for getting fired was because I would go on drinking binges and not show up to perform with the orchestra. I guess I did this to many times. After losing my job I decided to stay drunk, never sobering up at anytime that I can recall. When my money ran out I was unable to pay my rent. I didn't even have enough money to support my drinking habit." It was difficult to continue. "I was literally thrown out of my apartment with nothing but the shirt on my back. Everything else that I had owned I had sold to buy alcohol. Teresa, you have probably figured out that I am an alcoholic."

Teresa was sitting with a look of surprise and disbelief on her face. Nick continued with embarrassment, "Well at that point I couldn't buy any alcohol because I didn't have any money. I had no choice but to sober up a little. I started to realize that my life was going downhill. Reality hit me hard and suddenly I was terrified because I realized I had become a full-fledged bum. I didn't know what to do at that moment. What I wanted more than anything else in this world was a bottle to take me out of this reality even if it was just for the day.

"I had no choice but to wander through the miles of streets here in Philadelphia just trying to figure out how I was to survive. After a few weeks on the streets I was becoming a self-taught survival artist but I still had a lot to learn. A few more weeks and I had found a place that I would call home. It was a boarded up building where I shared the basement of the building with other street brothers.

"The only way I wanted to survive this life on the street was to stay drunk enough to be unconscious. It was the only way for me to cheat time in this brutal street life. After time passed I learned how to survive these harsh streets. To see me like that was not a pretty sight. If Sister Clara had seen me it would have broken her heart. This was not one of the chapters in life she had intended for me. Sister Clara worked so hard on me to teach me all the right paths and look what I had done to all of her hard work.

"So from day to day I wandered through the streets and alleys looking for little to eat and more to drink. One would have thought I was a zombie by my slow actions and the loss of control of my movements as the alcohol in my body was destroying my brain cells. My street brothers and I would gather together, share a bottle or two and drink to what we call loneliness after a hard day of rummaging through trash bins and garbage cans.

"The summer nights were cold and lonely but did not compare to the harsh winter nights, they were long and deathly cold. I have witnessed some of my street brothers freeze to death in their sleep. There were many winter nights when I was freezing and shaking uncontrollably from the cold that chilled me all the way to my bones. I felt that the street brothers who froze to death were the lucky ones at this point. I would wonder in those moments whether it was my time to leave this hellish life that I was leading. It would have been a blessing, when I would see the rising sun it only meant the starting of another gruesome day on the street. The days turned to months and then a year had gone by. I had established my own territory and had learned quite a bit about street living."

By now Teresa was showing her emotional reaction to this unbelievable episode of Nick's life on the street. Sniffles and tears were coming from Teresa as he continued with his story saying, "I missed playing the piano. Believe it or not but everything I was taught about the music was still fresh in my mind. If given an opportunity to play the piano, sober or drunk, I would have played my heart out.

"Some of the problems I encountered while living on the street were people spitting on me, calling me names, even occasionally shoves by the young hoodlums who got their kicks by beating up on me and other street brothers. There were a few times when I didn't make it back to my sleeping quarters because I had too much to drink and passed out in some alley. I would wake up in pain from a kick in the face or stomach by someone who just wanted something to kick. I don't know if they did it out of frustration or what their reasons they might have had.

"When one lives on the streets there are a few rules that one must follow and that is a street brother does not invade another's territory. There were many of fights when this rule was broken. In the beginning I had my share of fights and beatings. You learn even on the street to respect each other's property claims which consists of trash bins, eateries and sleeping quarters. If anyone crossed the property lines set up by someone else then they were met with serious consequences.

"There were a few exceptions to the rule. If several bums invaded your territory you had the choice of giving it up as a safe loss or taking on the whole bunch in a death wish which would have been an act of insanity. Some of us had to learn the hard way. But that's what being desperate for a drink will do, it makes you do senseless things out of desperation. There was always something in a trash bin that one could salvage to sell to get enough money for a drink.

"Street people see many things that the so-called normal people walking the streets do not see. I have seen people killing other people for little or no reason at all. I had a street friend that died because someone wanted to release their anger. Someone let their anger get out of control and injured him so that when they walked away they left a human being so critically injured that he later died pitifully in his sleep on a rundown half padded mattress in the basement he called home. I have also seen friends die from sickness, exposure or starvation."

Teresa, with tears streaming down her cheeks, broke into Nick's story saying, "Nick, this is so painful I don't know if I can stand listening to any more of this dreadful situation."

Nick calmly patted her hand, "I know it's hard for you to listen to this, but I need for you to hear it so you can understand more about me. This will answer some of the questions your curious mind has been wanting to ask me for along time. There is a reason for telling you about all of this. I will try and make my story as easy for you as I can. Please, Teresa, bear with me on this."

Teresa nodded her head with approval. After Nick went to get a Kleenex for her sniffling nose and teary eyes he continued, "This may sound barbaric but I literally had to fight off the stray dogs from the garbage cans behind some of the restaurants in order to get something to eat for my weak and trembling body. Some of the scars on my hands are from the bites of those dogs.

"During those years on the streets there were many days when I went into alcohol withdrawal because I couldn't meet my daily quota of money to buy the devil's brew. Some days when I did well at the trash bins my reward was getting enough money for a bottle. There were also times that not even the large garbage bins could supply my daily needs. Then I had no choice but to take to the streets and shamefully beg for handouts of loose change. Those were the times I hated the most.

"When I went out on the main streets begging for handouts, I tried to avoid looking at the big store front windows because every time I looked there was a reflection of this pitiful bum looking back at me. It was an unrecognizable image of a person that was in such a frightful condition that it literally scared the hell out of me. I would bow my head to plea for release to whomever my higher power would be. As I did my communicating to this higher power of mine the so-called normal people who heard me mumbling just thought I was jabbering senselessly. I would ask my higher power, why me? Why must I go on suffering like this day after day. I don't know how much more I can handle of this hellish life. I would be better off if you would just take me away from all this unnecessary daily struggle.

"At this point in time, I was no use to myself or anyone else. There certainly would have been one less eyesore on the city streets without my tarnished presence. I was wasting away on these streets."

While Nick had been talking the tears on Teresa's face had caused her makeup to dissolve and streak down her cheeks. It was hard for her to believe that the Nick she knew today was the same person he was discussing in his story.

Teresa took one of Nick's scarred hands and put it up to her cheek and just held it against the damp skin. She thought about what a hell of a nightmare this would have been if it had only been a dream. That it had been real was even worse. She had seen the scars on his hand as only adding to his character. But now she knew where these scars came from and what Nick had been through. While still holding Nick's hand up to her face she looked up with sorrowful eyes filled with love.

Nick looked back into her teary eyes. He was amazed at how beautiful her eyes were, even when they were wet with tears that brought out the blue color even more. Teresa broke his train of thoughts by saying, "It's hard to believe that you have gone through all that torment."

Nick decided to pause his story for a minute. He used this time to go into the other room to get a box of Kleenex for Teresa. He realized she would need them as she heard the rest of his story.

Teresa realized now why Nick's hands were so scarred. It was true that his story did answer many of her curious questions. Her heart ached with pain and sorrow from what she had just heard. She now knew why Nick would always stop to talk with the homeless, giving each a little contribution so that they could buy something to eat. She had never heard the conversations because she was afraid to get too close to the street people. She had always thought the donation was good-hearted of Nick, but deep inside she also thought it was a waste of money. Now she understands why Nick did these little acts of kindness.

Nick came back with the Kleenex. He sat down and glanced at Teresa with a smile and a twinkle in his eyes, silently letting her know that he was glad she was here with him. Then Nick proceeded with his story. "One day during this meaningless time of my life I was having a hard time finding anything to sell for the money I needed to buy my daily quota of alcohol. I was really hurting for a drink that day. I was so desperate that when a lady passed the bench where I was sitting her purse was too tempting. When she walked in front of me I grabbed the purse and ran as fast as I could. I wasn't fast enough to escape because I was caught red-handed a few blocks from where I had snatched the purse.

"I was taken to jail and put in a room that is called the bull pen. That's one big cell where thirty or more men stay temporarily until they were released on bail or brought into court. I waited several days for my court hearing. In those two days no one in the bull pen wanted to get near me because I smelled so bad and I was very sick from alcohol withdrawals. My hair was dirty and matted, my clothes were dirty and smelled rotten, even my shoes were covered with some things you wouldn't want to think about. I was shaking uncontrollably and at night I would go into a cold sweat and shiver through the night.

"When I finally got my trial date the prosecutor and judge were eager to get me out of the court room, so the judgement was rendered swiftly. My sentence was two years in prison which could be reduced to one year for good behavior.

"When I arrived at the prison I was the last person to get out of the bus, while everyone else practically ran out because of the stench I had created in the bus. After getting inside the prison walls, I was stripped and all of my clothes were put into a plastic bag for the trash. Everyone had some sarcastic oaths to shout at me. I took it all with my head hung low in disgrace. The prison doctor with the help of the security guards had to check everyone that came into the prison facility for any type of diseases. I was the only one that was not sent through the usual inspection because for they already knew I would have a variety of diseases. Before any of the guards would even touch me I was given a hard bristle brush and soap to use and sent to the showers. When I had finished taking my shower the guards were not satisfied with the results so I was sent back to the showers for the second time. I had to keep scrubbing with that brush that felt more like a wire brush that would be used to clean the grids of a barbecue grill.

"I stayed in the shower scrubbing two years of built-up dirt from my body until the guards felt I was clean enough for their satisfaction. When the scrubbing was over my skin was hurting so badly it was swollen and raw. I could hear the guards laughing at me, they wouldn't touch my hair to cut it until it was washed. The process of getting me cleaned up took four times longer than any other inmate. After that painful ordeal was over my hair was cut and I was put back in the shower just to rinse away the cut hair and anything else that clung onto it.

"Then came the moment for shaving. My face is one that will not grow a full beard but throughout the years of not shaving the area where it grew heavy enough to change the appearance of my face. After I was clean, shaved and had a hair cut the image I saw reflector in the mirror was still the same person I had seen in the store front windows. The pitiful looking face that I was staring at was mine. I could not believe that it was myself. The image that I kept in my mind for those two years was not to be that same face I was looking at.

"I had aged considerably in two years while living on the streets and had never noticed. While I was given medications for my diseases my head hung down in shame. I had literally wasted myself away. I could not help but cry as tears rolled down my aged and battered face."

Teresa was in tears now herself. "Oh Nick, oh Nick," she kept saying. "I am so sorry you had to go through all this. Please tell me that you are almost finished with your story. My heart can't take any more of this hellish nightmare, please tell me that you are almost finished with your story."

Nick gently pulled Teresa toward him and held her against his chest trying to comfort her by telling her, "I am getting close to the end of the gruesome part of my story."

10

Before resuming his story Nick took a Kleenex and gently started to dry Teresa's eyes and face. After a minutes rest, Teresa was ready for Nick to continue with his story. "The guards were shouting at me to hurry and quit wasting their time. After I was completely cleaned up, I was put into the prison's infirmary for medical care.

"The State of Pennsylvania was taking care of me now and being in the infirmary was many times better than living on the streets. I felt that I had walked out from the gates of Hell and back into the land of the living. In prison you were given three meals a day. Many of the prisoners complained about the quality of the food that to me was a feast. I used to feel badly that I knew there were people on the streets looking for anything edible while I was fed what I thought was a feast and the other ungrateful prisoners called it slop.

"If all those prisoners had been in my shoes just once, then they would consider what the prison facility served at meal times a rich man's meal. Life didn't seem fair. Just lying on a soft bed felt so remarkably good. One never appreciates what one has until it is gone. Something as simple as a soft bed was an example. It had been two years since I had slept on a soft mattress."

Teresa still sat teary-eyed and motionless as she listened with sadness to the story of pain that Nick had been through in his life. "Everyone follows a different path, sometimes the path is easy, sometimes it is hard," she thought.

Nick had arrived at the point of his story to describe his friend Mark who had shared his cell for the entire year. Mark had became his best friend during that time in prison. He described what he had done and what he had learned during that year.

Nick hesitated for a few seconds and then with a trembling voice said, "Sister Clara, someone so dear to me, passed away while I was serving time in prison. I was not even granted a furlough so that I could pay my last respects to the one person who had cared for me. She was the person who took me under her wing and believed in me. I was devastated because I couldn't go to her funeral. It took me awhile before I would forgive myself for getting into such a mess."

Nick could not control his emotions and finally after all these years let out a cry of guilt. This time Teresa grabbed Nick and pulled him towards her waiting shoulder as grief washed over him. When Nick again had control of his emotions he looked at Teresa and saw that they both were teary-eyed. Nick cleared his throat and said, "I must finish my story. I want to tell you something that is very important to me."

Nick continued with his story, "After leaving prison, I was fortunate to find a job at a music store. They were desperate for a salesperson in the piano department. I was there at the right time for a change. I was afraid they wouldn't hire me because of my prison record. But the music store never took time to check my background, because if they had, heaven only knew where I would be today. Luck was on my side for a change.

"The worst part of the story is over but I have a little more to tell you." Before Nick realized what happened Teresa quickly grabbed him and forced her way into his arms. With her arms clutched around his waist she hugged him with a slight squeeze to let him know how she felt about him. Nick responded by circling his arms around her and doing the same.

Teresa was still holding on to Nick when she looked up at him with large tear drops that lay on her cheeks. The lamplight reflected from the tears as she said to Nick, "I am so sorry you had to go through all of the pain and illnesses. No matter what you were, or even what you did, I love you enough to overlook any of these dreadful things. If you will give me the chance, I will show you that my love for you is forever."

The room was quiet as they remained wrapped in each others arms until they both had satisfied their need for consolation. With a small caress, as Nick brushed the hair from Teresa's cheek, the mood went from reassurance to passion. If the intensity of their emotions could have been measured by the gage for earthquakes the needle would have been flying off the Richter scale.

They both knew that this was not the moment to satisfy their passion and that they needed to take one step back and wait until their bodies cooled. The evening had passed during the intense conversation and they discovered that it was one o'clock in the morning. To give themselves time to regain their composure Nick headed for the kitchen to make fresh coffee. He asked Teresa if she wanted something to snack on. When she didn't answer he looked toward her to see her just sitting and staring into space in a daze.

Her mind was filled with everything Nick had revealed to her that night. She had been shocked to learn that the man she loved had lived in such conditions and had to endure such unnecessary pain and suffering. Teresa was amazed that he had been able to survive all that just to be the one who found his way into her heart. Fate had been responsible for sending Nick to her and she had been chosen because of her ability to love him and commit completely to him in return for his love.

"I have been in love with this man for a long time and tonight my love has grown even stronger," Teresa's thoughts were broken by the soft touch of Nick's hands as he touched her gently.

Nick spoke softly so that he didn't frighten Teresa out of her thoughts. "Come on honey, I have made more coffee and reheated this evening's leftovers."

Finally Teresa's eyes made contact with Nick's and she smiled, giving her face that bright glamorous glow which showed off her beauty. Then she said, "That sounds good. I'm both exhausted and hungry."

Very few words were spoken as they ate. It had been a difficult time for them both. Nick had relived the years that still haunted him. The hardest part was the disgrace and humiliation of revealing to Teresa his dreadful past. It had been difficult for Teresa to watch and listen to him describe his life. She had suffered again with him the pain and sorrow from his ordeal of surviving on the harsh streets. If that life hadn't been enough punishment it was climaxed with a year in the state's prison.

After they finished snacking, Nick looked at Teresa with guilt. He had not anticipated the amount of pain she would suffer from hearing his story. Her eyes were slightly swollen from crying. Hoping to ease her mind,

Nick took hold of her hand and softly said, "What I have left to tell you won't hurt. My story is almost over."

They left the table, this time leaving the dirty dishes behind, returned to the living room and took up their same seats. Nick wasted no time, "When I was growing up I had worked so hard on my music I had no time for anything else. Even though my music sat on the shelf collecting dust and my fingers were deprived from waltzing on the smooth surface of those ivory keys for two years on the street it was easy to regain the knowledge of the music I had studied for so many years.

"When the guards realized how much talent I had for playing the piano I was given special privileges so that I could practice more frequently. These were the same guards who were there when I arrived in the prison compound. They could not believe that the same bum they had to send back to the showers for the second time had this incredible gift. The guards were breaking prison rules by letting me practice because the prisoners were prohibited from having that much recreation time.

"Even with as much time as I spent practicing, I had a problem with my fingers. The years of abuse to my hands was now evident and I had lost some control of certain movements in my fingers. There were times when I would want my fingers to hit a certain key that I had chosen for particular tones and my fingers could not respond to my commands. Without those tones the musical piece was empty and incomplete.

"I would get so frustrated when my fingers did not respond to hit the right keys that I was afraid I had come to the end of my musical career. I sounded like the crazy man that I had been when I was living on the streets. I would talk to my fingers, better yet, I would curse at my fingers for not complying to my demands. But crazy or not, I was determined to win this battle. I felt that to much had already been lost.

"I vowed that not only would I play again, like I had before I began to drink but I would become even better. Besides, my thoughts of Sister Clara would not allow me to quit. Every time I would miss a key or note I would remember that she would always say, with so much patience, "OK Nicholas, let's start from the beginning and this time I want your full concentration."

"So I was practicing till my fingers hurt even more than they did when they were stepped on while I was living on the streets. But I welcomed the physical pain of practicing over the mental pain of memories from the past. It took some time to get my fingers under full control. With the condition that they were in I was truly grateful when my fingers came back to life and gave me another chance.

"Because music is my life it would have been a real blow for me if I had to find another career. The biggest disappointment that came out of this was that the appearance of my hands so shamefully scarred. But who was I to cry over hands that could still play the music of romance to broken hearts, play livelier tunes for the saddened and other delightful sounds of music to the eager listening ears. I was better off than the Phantom of the Opera. He had no choice but to mask his scarred face. I needed only but to cover my scarred hands with a pair of silk white gloves.

"Almost everything that I have put together to this day for my performance were ideas all thought of while I was in prison. Practicing day after day without missing even one, both while in prison and after prison, had paid off with a chance to perform. One day at work one of my co-workers learned that the pianist he had scheduled to play in his daughter's high school talent show canceled his appearance.

"The talent show was supposed to feature the students themselves from that school. All the coordinators for the program got together one day after school to discuss how they would get this show started. One of the coordinators suggested that it would be great if they could get a professional entertainer to come to the school and perform as a climax for the evening. They thought that watching a professional entertainer would encourage more students to perform and attract those students who did not perform to come and bring their parents.

"It was also understood that it was necessary for this professional entertainer to donate his or her time to the school. It seemed impossible but this coordinator was convinced that it could be done. Sam, who is one of my co-workers, has only one child, a daughter named Jeanie who was the student representative to the coordinators.

"Jeanie told everyone that she could probably get a professional pianist to perform in the talent show. Jeanie had heard her dad talking about a friend who was a professional pianist and who happened to owe him a big favor. After everything was put together for the school's program and the schedules were printed with the list of performers this friend of Sam's called him to say that he would be unable to perform because of an error in his scheduling.

"Sam was furious. I overheard him because he was practically shouting about how his friend had let him down. He was telling one of the co-workers about it in our break room. I thought that this was a golden opportunity to activate my plans.

"I was desperate enough to consider performing at a high school without payment. But the way I saw it, one had to start from the bottom. I just wanted to get a start and take my chances from there. So this magnificent and incredible character "Charlee" was brought into existence. Teresa, I am both Charlee's creator and Charlee himself."

With a swift cry of joy Teresa launched herself onto Nick's lap embracing him she said, "I can't believe it, I just can't believe it." Again tears fell down her cheeks as her overwhelming joy was expressed. As Teresa sat on Nick's lap, she vowed never to indicate to Nick that his secret had already been guessed. Nick had made one mistake in his attempt to keep the character of Charlee anonymous that she had used to support her suspicion that Nick and Charlee were the same person. Now she had a secret of her own that she would never reveal. This was another indication of her devotion.

Teresa was comfortable sitting on Nick's lap so she remained there as he continued with his story. "After finally convincing Sam that I knew a pianist that would be happy to perform at his daughter's high school he asked me to obtain this pianist to perform at the talent show. I wanted to shout with joy. Somehow, I felt that Sister Clara had a hand in this. I felt blessed to have been given a chance when I was beginning to think that my chances of performing were a thing of the past.

"I didn't want to disappoint Sam. I kept telling myself, don't blow it. I promised myself that my performance would be my best. As crazy as this may sound, I had so much confidence that I made a bet with Charlee that I would be asked to perform again." Teresa listened to Nick with amazement. "I remember," said Nick, "the very first time I was dressed up as Charlee was the evening you saw me in the elevator. I was headed to my first performance and I thought you were trying to recognize the person behind the makeup. When you didn't recognize me I knew that Charlee would successfully hide my identity."

Nick took a breath and looked into Teresa's eyes, "You were beautiful that evening in the elevator. Your face was an extra inspiration for me to do well. I can't explain it, you must just believe me."

Teresa had wondered several times throughout the evening why Nick was telling her his life story. He had answered many of the questions she had asked in her mind. Now Nick answers that unspoken question as well, "My reason for revealing all my dark secrets is because I want you to know everything about me before I ask you an important question. I want to create a bond of trust between us. I don't want you to have any doubts." Teresa's puzzled mind began to spin as Nick continued, "I want us to be able to depend on each other no matter what the circumstances are and I want us both to be there for each other when the time comes.

"I had decided to look for a partner that I could trust completely. Part of my plan was to reveal everything that I have told you. I wanted my partner to be able to trust me.

"Do you trust me, Teresa?"

11

In a low smooth voice Nick said, "Charlee and I would love to have you become our partner in my musical career."

Teresa held her hands over her mouth now letting out a soft cry as her lips quivered. When she was able to speak, all she was able to say was, "Oh, Nick." Then she had to pause for a minute to compose herself. When the sniffling eased she repeated, "Oh Nick, I would love to be your partner." With tears streaming down her lovely face she placed her arms around him again and leaned weakly against his chest. This was too much excitement for one evening.

"Hold on, Teresa. I haven't finished yet" After the excitement eased, Nick said with some concern. "You know Teresa. I am twenty-seven years old and I have lived without a female companion throughout my adult life. I wake up alone each morning but I would love to share the dawn with someone special.

"Each day when I leave for work I am content with my life only because of where I am now compared to my past. Deep down when I am alone I know that there is something missing from my life. My day is mixed with the new faces of customers and the familiar faces of the people I work with.

"After my day of work is finished, I walk down to the corner café and have my usual coffee before I order something to eat. There I sit by myself again with no one to share the evening's meal. I can't share anything that happened during the day. There is no laughter or exchange of words around my table.

"The only sound heard coming from my table is the sound of a spoon hitting my bowl of soup every once in a while or the sound of a knife against my plate after it slices through my meat. After satisfying my hunger pains, I leave for home. I entered the cafe alone and so I leave alone, content only with what I have eaten.

"But inside there is still a hunger that can't be satisfied with food. I have been patiently waiting to satisfy this kind of hunger. When I get to my apartment and the door opens there is nothing but darkness and cold silence in my apartment. What keeps me from going out of my mind is that I look forward to sitting down at the piano. I can always find music that will lift my spirits from even the gloomiest moment.

"Teresa," said Nick, "I am tired of being alone. I would love to fill this emptiness in my life. I hope that I will be able to do the same for someone else." Teresa was sitting quietly. She was still dazed from the thrill of Nick's request to become his partner. She has no clue to what Nick is about to do.

Nick continued by saying, "What's missing in my life today is the one ingredient to ease this hunger pain. You are the missing ingredient Teresa. I would love to have you as my partner for life.

"Teresa, I am asking if you marry me and be the love of my life forever." Nick's ears should have been shattered by the ecstatic scream that come from Teresa.

In a softer voice she repeated, "Yes, yes I will marry you Nick." This was to be one of the greatest moment of their lives. Their ears were now filled with the music only lovers could hear. Each had waited for the moment when Nick finally made his move towards Teresa's lips. It seemed like an eternity passed before the magical moment of contact was made.

The kiss that landed on Teresa's lips was as soft as the touch of a butterfly as it started a tingling sensation of passion that sent signals of arousal all through her body adding to her appetite for passion. This butterfly kiss on her ravenous lips tasted to him like the sweetest nectar of love adding a greater invitation for more of Nick's soft sensational butterfly kisses.

The kissing compelled them past the boundaries that had kept them separate. There was no longer a reason to hold back from fulfilling their needs. Visions of fireworks filled their minds as their kissing and lovemaking progressed. Nothing could have parted them from each other.

Lingering in the air was the symphony of love heard in the early morning's light by the two people who were deeply in love. The dawn shone it's blessing on this union of true love between man and woman as Nick and his bride-to-be shared the special time together.

• • •

Nick and Teresa were married secretly in Mexico. They took extra precautions to ensure that he was established as her husband before she began her work as

Charlee's agent and partner. After a few weeks had passed as man and wife they began their professional union with two engagements.

The first program was Nick's third appearance at a Philadelphia high school. They had both decided that this would be Charlee's last free performance for the schools. With Teresa working as an agent for Charlee she could actively solicit new engagements. They hoped to schedule several performances for Charlee to entertain the people who had been waiting for an opportunity to see him.

Teresa had the ambition and dedication to her new career as Charlee's agent-partner to find many places for him to perform. The second engagement would be the opening of the mall built by Mr. Brenner's real estate company. Teresa called Mr. Brenner and introduced herself as Charlee's agent to discuss the plans for the mall's entertainment.

Teresa's first experience as Charlee's partner would be to assist his performance at the high school. She was overwhelmed by the reaction of the audience. Their faces looked at Charlee with amazement as they paid rapt attention to the sounds of harmony that came from the piano. Nick's hands, even with their deformities, masterfully sought the right notes for their hungry ears to absorb.

The emotions Teresa felt created a lump in her throat. She was delighted to be a partner in this exciting business with Nick. As she watched him perform, disguised as Charlee, she thought how lucky she was to be in love with a man who treated her like a princess. She was certain that his affections were devoted completely to her but wondered how she had won his love.

Teresa looked forward to the day she would bear Nick's children. His child would be a permanent gift of himself. She knew that they would need to concentrate on Charlee's career for several years before they could have any children.

Teresa had already shown progress as an agent. She had contacted the media and arranged for representatives to be at both the school and at the shopping mall. Amazingly she even had media from out-of-state requesting directions to come to the school for an interview with this rising new star of Philadelphia.

Prior to Charlee's appearance, the introduction included the announcement that tonight was Charlee's last performance at the schools. At the conclusion of Charlee's performance that evening the audience went wild with a standing ovation which lasted almost three minutes. Teresa could not help but shed a few tears for such evidence of approval given by the audience.

It took Charlee almost an hour and a half after the end of the program just to leave the school gym. Many fans blocked his exit as they sought autographs. Other fans wanted only to get a closer look at this magnificent entertainer. Both Nick and Teresa were gratified to know that there were so many fans, young and old, in Philadelphia who loved Charlee. Most of his recognition and popularity in such a short time was due to the attention of the media.

Part of that time had been spent in an interview with the media. The TV crews and newspaper photographers took pictures of Charlee from every angle. The out-of-state reporters appeared surprised and amazed by his performance. Charlee fortunately had a beautiful agent that interpreted his comments.

Exhausted from the evening of entertainment, Nick and Teresa headed for home. The cab delivered Teresa to the apartment building. Charlee remained inside as the cab headed away. This was planned as a decoy so that no one would suspect the relationship between Nick, Teresa and Charlee.

When Nick arrived home later he approached Teresa as she sat resting her tired body on the couch. "What do you think about the performance this evening?"

"This evening was so exciting," Teresa said, expressing herself. "I am still so excited I feel like I'm on cloud nine and I won't come down for a long time. I can't explain all of my reactions. Your performance was overwhelming."

Nick sat down beside Teresa and gently gave her a kiss. Teresa returned the kiss and Nick wrapped his arms around her warm, soft and tender body and said with a smile, "My dear, you did an excellent job. You don't know how much it meant to me to have you there to help. Thank you, love."

Preparations were being made for the engagement at the shopping mall. Two days before the grand opening, Teresa took time off from her work at the library to go to the mall. As Charlee's agent she wanted to make sure that everything would be ready for him. When she located the area where he would perform she was happy to notice that everything was in place and waiting for Charlee. A Steinway grand piano sat waiting his presence.

As Teresa walked toward the grand piano, her footsteps echoed throughout the mall. The huge tri-level mall was beautifully designed with the center of the mall formed around a huge circular opening which was specially designed for entertainment. The circular walkways on all three floors had railings for safety and yet were designed so that one could stand and watch the entertainment. Benches had been provided for anyone with the leisure time to sit and watch the entertainment. The second level would be the best place for observation. This was the level where the food court was located with tables and chairs set around the circular walkway. The customers would be encouraged to eat and relax while watching the performances.

Teresa looked around to make sure that everything was positioned correctly. After she had checked the lights and the sound equipment she stood by the magnificent piano and stared at it for some time. Then without any hesitation, she pulled the bench away from underneath this handsomely designed Steinway and sat in front of the keyboard. Her fingers were sliding over the glossy finish while she sat admiring the Steinway in its perfection. Her pretty face smiled back in the polished reflection from the surface.

Her hands moved down and with one finger she gently brushed across the shiny ivory keys. She felt a lump of excitement in her throat. Teresa tried to swallow the lump but she was compelled toward an unexplainable occurrence. As she sat on the bench, her eyes suddenly closed as she went deep into thought. The emotions that captured her body gave Teresa the image of blood, full of energetic enzymes, flowing rapidly through her veins. The feeling was so warm and soothing that it left her body limply relaxed but yet charged with the energetic feeling of excitement.

As Teresa sat there, overpowered by this wonderful feeling, she turned to sit in a playing position. With her eyes still closed she slowly raised her hands, holding them in midair for a few seconds. In those few seconds there was almost complete silence except for the little noise coming from store employees still trying to get their shops ready for the grand opening. Then like a cobra striking its target, Teresa's fingers struck the keys filling this mall with music.

Her mind was in a transcendent state of being and she felt as if her soul was floating. Teresa was practically in a hypnotic trance that almost explained the way she performed on the piano. One would have thought that Charlee had come to practice for the grand opening. When the few store employees working in the mall heard the music coming from the grand piano they stopped what they were doing to follow the sounds coming from this masterfully built Steinway. The music echoed throughout the mall with an acoustic sound so impressive that a number of curious people stopped working as they listened to Teresa play.

Teresa was unaware that she had a curious and appreciative audience. Her performance was indeed very good, in fact it was good enough to attract attention. Teresa's musical selections were well chosen. Her performance lasted half-hour.

Her captive audience was curious about the identity of this fantastic pianist. Some thought of the possibility that Charlee had come to practice. They all knew that Charlee was to perform for the grand opening. Most of the audience knew that Charlee's disguise included a wish not to reveal whether the character was male or female. Teresa was not aware that they were considering her presence as the solution to the puzzle of Charlee's identity. Nor did it occur to her that they would start the rumors that Charlee was female.

When Teresa finished her performance she was startled from her state of mystical absorption by the applause coming from her appreciative audience as someone above her shouted, "Bravo, Bravo." She was overwhelmed to the crowd that had gathered while she had been lost in her music. Her eyes and mind had been closed to her surroundings while she had performed.

"Are you Charlee?" one man asked as he walked up to Teresa.

She smiled her special smile and answered, "Oh no, I'm Charlee's agent. I just came to check to see if everything was ready for the grand opening."

"Well the way you played, lady, I certainly thought that you were Charlee," he replied.

"Thank you," Teresa blushed as she said to the man, "You really need to listen to Charlee a little closer, then you will notice the difference between us. There is truly a big difference. But I thank you for your compliment." She gave one last glance at the equipment to reassure herself for the last time that everything was setup satisfactorily and left the mall.

As she headed home in the cab, she wondered about her strange experience at the mall. What had driven her to play the piano. And why hadn't she noticed anyone while she was playing? "Strange" That was the word to describe her experience. Her final thought on the subject was to wonder if this was an omen of some kind.

Nick and Teresa did extremely well at the mall. It was a profitable day for them as well as the new shops at the mall.

• • •

As the years went by, Teresa adjusted to her position as Charlee's agent. Nick had chosen his partner wisely. She was eventually able to quit her job as a librarian and devote all of her time to promoting and scheduling concerts for Charlee to perform.

The citizens of Philadelphia were fortunate when Charlee performed many concerts throughout the city. The mayor's prediction when he first saw Charlee perform, stating that a new star would be born right here in their city of Philadelphia, became a reality. His fame and popularity spread through the rest of the country as he appeared on many national shows and TV concerts. Teresa continued to stand by his side in her position as Charlee's voice.

Charlee's fame and fortune grew. Following their sixth wedding anniversary they were able to achieve their most glorious goal, Teresa gave birth to a son who they named Clark Kristifer. They had both thought seriously about choosing the right name for their son. Nick chose the first name as Clark because it was a male version of the first four letters to Sister Clara's first name. Kristifer was the name chosen by Teresa because that was her father's name.

Between concerts and traveling, Nick continued to give Teresa piano lessons. As Clark grew, he was included with lessons of his own started at an early age in life. Nick had a subtle reason for encouraging Clark's lessons. As any proud father, he wanted his son to follow in his footsteps and excel in the study of the piano.

Even after the years of lessons Teresa had received from her husband, Nick continued to push her to increase her skill and experience on the piano. He wanted her to become the best pianist she could be. He considered it insurance in the event that anything were to happen to him.

He explained to Teresa his reasons, as both husband and father, for insisting on the lessons. "I know it is hard on you to take lessons because of your busy schedule. But trust me, dear, it is important for you to take these lessons." Teresa did not view the interruption to her busy schedule as a hardship. She had always looked forward to those lessons as time to relax with her husband's undivided attention.

As his father, Nick's goal was to teach Clark Kristifer as much as possible. He wanted Clark to continue his education through college to go beyond his own skill.

12

As the years passed the family crossed the United States many times with concert tours. As his reputation grew Charlee received invitations from other countries outside the USA. Nick and Teresa were happy to accept the opportunities to travel and decided to schedule performances in some of the foreign countries just so they could see other parts of the world. Charlee was becoming well known the world over.

Nick and Teresa had been married for sixteen years and they were as much in love today as they had been at the beginning. Each foreign tour was like a honeymoon trip. One day during one of these trips, Nick was feeling ill and Teresa persuaded him to see a doctor. The foreign doctor told Teresa that Nick was very ill and needed to be hospitalized to have some tests done. He did not reveal his suspicions because he did not want to alarm them.

Teresa wanted to have Nick treated in an American hospital so she cancelled all the remaining concerts that had been scheduled throughout the foreign countries and headed back to the USA. She did not cancel any of the American concert invitations because she did not know what to expect from the illness that had overcome

Nick. She felt that when Nick recovered he could continue with the concerts that had been scheduled.

The news from the test results was not good. Nick's liver was in complete failure from his years of drinking. As Nick and Teresa held hands the doctor told them he possibly had two weeks left to live. Teresa broke into uncontrollable tears as Nick held and cradled her in his arms and tried to comfort her. She continued to cry through the night.

This was to be the hardest and most devastating time in Teresa's life. Clark Kristifer was not aware of his father's prognosis. That would come soon enough. Teresa had to hire a nanny to care for him while she spent many hours in the hospital with Nick.

Nick thought that it would be best if he had a talk with Clark to explain the future. Nick talked to Clark about life and death. Those few hours became a part of the son's most precious moments as Nick prepared Clark for the heart breaking separation. Nick explained to his son that he could be strong and still be able to cry. That in his tears he could find the strength within himself to carry on and watch over his mother. Now he would be the man of the house but that his mother would still be head of the house, in other words the boss.

At the end of their long discussion, Nick opened a box and handed to Clark his battered and aged harmonica. He told Clark that had been his first musical instrument. He asked Clark to keep it for him. Surprisingly, Clark Kristifer took it a lot better than Teresa thought he would. It was probably because of the gentle way that Nick had explained it to him.

Teresa was able to have Nick spend the time he had remaining at home. That was where Nick wanted to be when he passed on. He wanted only to be with his family in the privacy of their home.

Nick and Teresa spent many hours holding hands and talking about the past, the present and the future. There was a lot of talk about how Teresa would work on being strong.

"I feel bad that I am abandoning you, leaving you and Clark to face the future alone. Yet I know how strong a woman and mother you are." Nick tried hard to lift Teresa's spirits.

Teresa spent her time trying to make Nick as comfortable as possible in his last hours. She assured him that she would be strong for their son Clark Kristifer. Their son was now a young man of ten, going on twenty. Hours ticked away as their talk became strenuous whispers. Nick expressing himself told Teresa, "You and I have always been so happy together. You were my life and my inspiration, you were always the first music to me."

The moment Teresa had dreaded became a reality as Nick started to fade away. Teresa could see it coming and squeezed his hand as he struggled to open his eyes for the last time. He wanted to get one last glimpse of his lovely wife of sixteen years. He smiled his last and asked Teresa in a faint voice to show him that special smile of hers. He said that he wanted to take that special smile with him. Teresa could not restrain the tears that were pouring uncontrollably from her blood-shot eyes as she forced herself, for the sake of her beloved husband, to give Nick that special smile with those magnificent deep dimples he cherished so much.

It was dreadfully hard for Teresa to smile. A weak but loving squeeze came from Nick as he struggled, "I love you…" were the last words he said.

Teresa's loud cry of sorrow echoed through the house. "Nick, Ooooh Nick," then silence. Teresa thought the sound of a faint and lonely cry from the strings of a single weeping violin echoed softly in the saddened house that entombing the lifeless body of Nick. The music sounded like the saddest of emotions which only a violin could express so well. But this violin could only be heard by Teresa.

Epilogue

Three months after Nick's passing Teresa had been struggling to get herself and her son's life back together. She still found it hard to accept the idea that Nick was really gone from her life in form, but she knew that he would always be with her in spirit. She also knew that Nick wanted her to be strong. She had been blessed with sixteen wonderful years married to such a kind and giving man. He was a man any woman would want to have had in her life. Teresa paused with her thoughts for a moment, and gave herself enough time to control the almost overwhelming need to cry.

Her current goal was to regain her composure and devote herself to the challenge of raising her son, Clark Kristifer. In the days and months to come Clark would surely miss his father very much. Even though Nick was very busy he had always found time to be with Clark. The boy had inherited his father's gifted talent as a pianist.

For a ten-year old, Clark played the piano exceptionally well. Their son was the most precious gift Nick had left to Teresa. Clark was a visible part of his father. Nick had spent years teaching both his wife and his son how to play the piano with the same passion he had possessed. This would be a special memory that they would carry in their hearts throughout their lives.

Teresa was amazed that together she and Nick had been successful in disguising his identity for years. Now one of her jobs was to cancel all of the future engagements scheduled for Charlee.

Six months after Nick's death a program was advertised at the concert hall on Seventh Avenue and 57th Street in New York City. This was the home of the New York Philharmonic and where some of the world's finest musicians had performed, like Vladimir Horowitz, Jan Paderewski and many others. This address was known as Carnegie Hall. It was evident that an important event was about to happen because limousines were constantly pulling in and out of the traffic in front of Carnegie Hall to drop off their passengers. Attending the concert was the Vice President of the United States with members of the White House Cabinet right behind him.

Who could be performing this evening that was so popular to interest these important people? On the marquee board over the entrance of the concert hall in big bold letters for all to see the sign read:

THIS EVENING'S ENGAGEMENT IS THE
MASTERFUL PIANIST AND ENTERTAINER
"CHARLEE"

and underneath all this, it was marked, SOLD OUT. What could have happened? Teresa was supposed to have cancelled this engagement at Carnegie Hall with all of the other performances. If she had forgotten this engagement then she proved that she was only human. After all, look what she had been through these past months.

This concert hall was one of Nick's favorite places to perform so Charlee had been scheduled here many times in the past. Teresa had been looking forward to being here again. She had thought of this concert hall as having a character in itself because of its long history of great musicians. Charlee had also become known as one of the greatest musicians among those who have entertained here at Carnegie Hall.

Right now the problem appeared to be that Teresa had not remembered to call and cancel Charlee's performance. For several months that had been a painful duty. She had worked hard to fill Nick's schedule with invitations for Charlee to perform. Events had been scheduled even up to a year and a half in advance, proving her ability as an excellent agent. She had planned two months earlier to cancel this engagement.

Carnegie Hall was filled with people from every class. Representative from the upper wealthy class of people rubbed elbows with taxi drivers and housewives. Everyone who had been able to buy a ticket for tonight's entertainment had come to watch Charlee. The sound of voices all clashing with each other made it hard to understand anything that was said. It would be a disappointment to all of them when the announcer came on the stage to inform them that this show was to be cancelled at the last minute.

What was Teresa doing? Did she know what was happening here at the concert hall? Will she be devastated because she had forgotten to cancel this engagement? She really didn't need any more problems at this point in her life.

Certainly the announcer will appear soon to cancel the concert. The audience would be provoked to show their disapproval by shouts of obscenities and whatever helped them to release the anger of their disappointment. The announcer appeared and walked across the stage floor toward the microphone. He began, "Ladies and Gentlemen, this evening we have a performer who really needs no introduction. This artist has a unique and talented way of performing and is known especially for his magical fingers on the piano. This entertainer has been requested to perform the world over. We are fortunate to have him with us this evening. And now Ladies and Gentlemen, I give you Charlee."

The applause coming from the audience is loud and crisp. When the announcer walked off the stage it was left bare for several minutes. The impatient audience began to mumble and become restless. A couple of more seconds went by as the mumbling became louder. A shout came from someone in the audience, "Hey Charlee where are you." Then slowly from behind the stage curtains walked a person dressed in Charlee's outfit.

Who could be this imposter? As this imitation Charlee walked onto the stage the relieved audience again gave their applause. How could this happen? There on stage stood the spitting image of Charlee. Who did Teresa get to fill in Charlee's shoes? It was amazing to watch as this imposter performed in a manner identical to Charlee's.

When the time came for the piano performance it was simply unbelievable as well. Could it be possible that Charlee had left Nick in his grave to come back and perform this evening? No, we all know that is impossible don't we? The musical pieces played this evening had all been strictly classical. The imposter had given as superb a performance as Charlee had always done in the past. The audience believed that Charlee had been performing this evening.

At the end of the performance, Charlee received a standing ovation. The curtains rolled down and as always the curtains rolled up for the second time for Charlee to give his second bow. This pianist and entertainer was an imposter that had fooled everyone into believing that Charlee had performed for them. But that was because they had never known the true identity of Charlee so they would never know of Charlee's death.

As Charlee was giving the final bow of appreciation to the audience a slight difference in the facial outline could have been seen by only the most astute eye. This person had a profile which was slightly slimmer than Charlee's facial outline. As the character who had portrayed Charlee all evening took the final bow, the smile that was given was that special smile with those deep enchanting dimples. Charlee lived on.

THE END

ABOUT THE AUTHOR

Nicholas Lawrence Portillo, Jr. was born February 5, 1946 in Albuquerque New Mexico. He was two and a half years old when his mother passed away. So he was put in the orphanage and lived there until he was around nine years old. He was sent back home to live with his father and stepmother. He comes from a poor family, living in a poor community. He never finished school. He lived a hard life, and that's what brought him to writing this novel. He had never finished anything in his life. So writing this novel brings closer to all the unfinished circumstances in life. So for those who have always wanted to write, if I can do it, so can you.

www.ingramcontent.com/pod-product-compliance
Ingram Content Group UK Ltd.
Pitfield, Milton Keynes, MK11 3LW, UK
UKHW040015200726
13854UKWH00001B/216

9 781403 340986